POKÉMON

SINNOH HANDBOOK

SCHOLASTIC INC.

New York   Toronto   London   Auckland   Sydney
Mexico City   New Delhi   Hong Kong   Buenos Aires

ISBN-13: 978-0-545-00072-7

ISBN-10: 0-545-00072-6

PUBLISHED BY SCHOLASTIC INC.

12 11 10 9 8 7 6 5 4 3 2   7 8 9 10 11 12/0

DESIGNED BY DIRTY BANDITS

PRINTED IN THE U.S.A.

FIRST PRINTING, SEPTEMBER 2007

POKÉMON

SINNOH HANDBOOK

BY TRACY WEST
AND KATHERINE NOLL

A WHOLE NEW WORLD OF POKÉMON

Have you memorized the name of every single Pokémon? Do you know their types and Evolutions by heart? Well, you'd better ask your Alakazam if you can borrow some brain power. There's a bunch of brand new Pokémon in town!

In this book you will learn about the Pokémon that live in the Sinnoh region of the Pokémon world. Some of them are Pokémon you've seen before. But most of them are Pokémon you've never met.

We've listed them alphabetically so that you can easily find the Pokémon you're looking for. Each entry has useful information about that Pokémon.

HERE'S WHAT YOU'LL FIND ON EACH PAGE:

NAME
SPECIES OF POKÉMON

- **HOW TO SAY IT:**
  Let's face it, most Pokémon names are pretty unusual. We've broken up the spelling of each name syllable by syllable.

- **POSSIBLE MOVES:**
  Each Pokémon has a special set of moves that it can use in battle. In this book we'll show you some of the moves that a Pokémon can learn as it gains more experience.

- **TYPE:**
  Every Pokémon is associated with one or more types. There are 17 different types: Fire, Grass, Water, Normal, Electric, Bug, Ghost, Flying, Fighting, Psychic, Steel, Rock, Ground, Ice, Poison, Dark, and Dragon. A Pokémon can be a combination of two different types. This is called a dual-type Pokémon.

- **HEIGHT / WEIGHT**

- **EVOLUTION CHAIN:**
  If the Pokémon has an evolved form or pre-evolved form, we'll show you its place in the chain.

- **WE'LL ALSO TELL YOU SOME INTERESTING FACTS ABOUT EACH POKÉMON!**

NOW THAT YOU KNOW HOW TO USE THIS BOOK, GET OUT THERE AND EXPLORE! EVERY NEW POKÉMON REPRESENTS A BRAND NEW ADVENTURE JUST WAITING FOR YOU.

WELCOME TO THE SINNOH REGION

The Pokémon world is divided into regions. In each region you'll find different Pokémon to catch, different kinds of competitions to enter, and different Trainers and Pokémon experts.

Ash and his friends have explored the regions of Kanto, Johto, and Hoenn. Now they're on they're way to a new region: the land of Sinnoh. It's a lush and beautiful place with lots of new and exciting Pokémon to discover.

Trainers in the Sinnoh region begin their journey in Twinleaf Town. They report to Professor Rowan, a leading Pokémon expert. He gives them a choice of three starter Pokémon: Turtwig, a Grass-type; Chimchar, a Fire-type; or Piplup, a Water-type.

Once a Trainer's journey begins, there are many places to explore in Sinnoh. There are Rock-and-Ground-type Pokémon to be found in the hills and mountains. The lakes in Sinnoh are teeming with Water-types, as well as the sea that surrounds this island region. The leafy forests are home to Grass-type Pokémon. And like every region in the Pokémon world, there are towns and cities with new Trainers to battle.

Ash and his friends have plenty of adventures in store for them as they journey through Sinnoh—and so do you! Just make sure you have this book with you to help you as you explore.

ABOMASNOW

FROST TREE POKÉMON

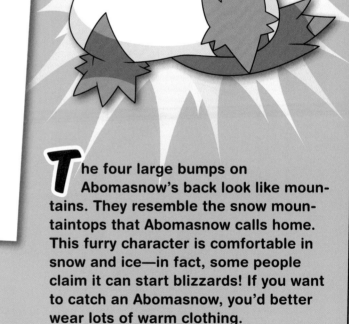

The four large bumps on Abomasnow's back look like mountains. They resemble the snow mountaintops that Abomasnow calls home. This furry character is comfortable in snow and ice—in fact, some people claim it can start blizzards! If you want to catch an Abomasnow, you'd better wear lots of warm clothing.

SNOVER   ABOMASNOW

ABRA

HOW TO SAY IT:
AB-ruh

POSSIBLE MOVES:
Teleport

TYPE:
Psychic

HEIGHT:
2' 11"

WEIGHT:
43.0 lbs.

If you ever encounter an Abra, chances are it'll be sleeping. This Pokémon snoozes 18 hours a day to reserve its psychic energy. But just because it's not awake doesn't mean it's helpless. If Abra senses danger, it can Teleport without waking up!

REMEMBER WHEN . . .
. . . Ash battled spooky Gym Leader Sabrina? Her Abra battled Pikachu without waking up! Then Abra evolved into Kadabra—and Sabrina won the battle!

ABRA   KADABRA   ALAKAZAM

AIPOM

LONG TAIL POKÉMON

HOW TO SAY IT:
AY-pom

POSSIBLE MOVES:
Scratch, Tail Whip, Sand-Attack, Astonish, Baton Pass, Tickle, Fury Swipes, Swift, Screech, Agility

TYPE: Normal

HEIGHT: 2' 07"

WEIGHT: 25.4 lbs.

Aipom's tail is almost like an extra arm. It can reach out and grab Aipom's favorite food, fruit. Maybe this is what gives this Pokémon so much energy. Aipom can keep dodging an opponent's attack until it tires out!

AIPOM   AMBIPOM

ALAKAZAM

PSYCHIC POKÉMON

HOW TO SAY IT:
al-uh-kuh-ZAM

POSSIBLE MOVES:
Teleport, Kinesis, Confusion, Disable, Psybeam, Reflect, Recover, Future Sight, Calm Mind, Psychic, Trick, Miracle Eye, Psycho Cut

TYPE: Psychic

HEIGHT: 4' 11"

WEIGHT: 105.8 lbs.

A combination of super intelligence and psychic powers makes this Pokémon hard to beat. With an IQ of 5,000, and a brain like a supercomputer, Alakazam can remember every battle it's ever fought — and just about everything else.

ABRA   KADABRA   ALAKAZAM

AMBIPOM

LONG TAIL POKÉMON

HOW TO SAY IT:
AM-bih-pom

POSSIBLE MOVES:
Scratch, Tail Whip, Sand-Attack, Astonish, Baton Pass, Tickle, Fury Swipes, Swift, Screech, Agility, Double Hit, Fling, Nasty Plot, Last Resort

TYPE:
Normal

HEIGHT:
3' 11"

WEIGHT:
44.8 lbs.

If you're an Ambipom, two tails are better than one! Especially if each tail has three fingers on it that are great for grabbing things. Out in the wild, you are likely to see a lot of Ambipom traveling together. They form big tribes, and they like to link their tails together to form a circle of friendship.

AIPOM   AMBIPOM

AZELF

HOW TO SAY IT:
AZZ-elf

POSSIBLE MOVES:
Rest, Imprison, Detect, Confusion, Uproar, Future Sight, Nasty Plot, Extrasensory, Last Resort, Natural Gift, Explosion

TYPE:
Psychic

HEIGHT:
1' 00"

WEIGHT:
0.7 lbs.

Azelf is part of a new trio of Legendary Pokémon, along with Uxie and Mesprit. This mysterious Pokémon has the power to control someone's will. Azelf can make you stop doing something, or make you do the same thing over and over! That's a pretty strong power for a tiny Pokémon.

DOES NOT EVOLVE

AZUMARILL
AQUA RABBIT POKÉMON

HOW TO SAY IT:
ah-ZOO-mare-ill

POSSIBLE MOVES:
Tackle, Defense Curl, Tail Whip, Water Gun, Rollout, Double-Edge, Bubblebeam, Rain Dance, Hydro Pump

TYPE: *Water*
HEIGHT: *2' 07"*
WEIGHT: *62.8 lbs.*

This good-natured Pokémon spends almost all of its time in the water. That's why it has a bubble pattern on its lower body. It helps to camouflage Azumarill from predators.

AZURILL **MARILL** **AZUMARILL**

AZURILL
POLKA DOT POKÉMON

HOW TO SAY IT:
ah-ZOO-rill

POSSIBLE MOVES:
Splash, Charm, Tail Whip, Bubble, Slam, Water Gun

TYPE: *Normal*
HEIGHT: *0' 08"*
WEIGHT: *4.4 lbs.*

Azurill's blubbery, bouncy tail is this Pokémon's most interesting feature. It holds all the nutrients this little creature needs to grow. It can also spin its tail like a lasso, hurl it, and then send its own body flying long distances!

AZURILL **MARILL** **AZUMARILL**

BARBOACH

HOW TO SAY IT:
bar-BOACH

POSSIBLE MOVES: Mud Slap, Mud Sport, Water Sport, Water Gun, Mud Bomb, Amnesia, Water Pulse, Magnitude, Rest, Snore, Earthquake, Future Sight, Fissure, Aqua Tail

TYPE: Water-Ground

HEIGHT: 1' 04"

WEIGHT: 4.2 lbs.

This Pokémon can be found in muddy waters. It buries itself in the mud but leaves its whiskers exposed so they can detect prey swimming by. If a foe tries to grab Barboach, a slimy film on its body will help this Pokémon slip away.

BARBOACH → **WHISCASH**

BEAUTIFLY

BUTTERFLY POKÉMON

HOW TO SAY IT:
BUE-tee-fly

POSSIBLE MOVES:
Absorb, Gust, Stun Spore, Morning Sun, Mega Drain, Whirlwind, Attract, Silver Wind, Giga Drain, Bug Buzz

TYPE: Bug-Flying

HEIGHT: 3' 03"

WEIGHT: 62.6 lbs.

If you want to spy a Beautifly, find a pretty flower on a spring day and wait patiently. Chances are a Beautifly will fly by, eager to sap up the tasty pollen with its long, thin mouth.

WURMPLE → **SILCOON** → **BEAUTIFLY**

BASTIODON

HOW TO SAY IT:
BAS-tee-oh-don

POSSIBLE MOVES:
Tackle, Protect, Taunt, Metal Sound, Take Down, Iron Defense, Swagger, AncientPower, Block, Endure, Metal Burst, Iron Head, Taunt

TYPE:
Rock-Steel

HEIGHT:
4' 03"

WEIGHT:
329.6 lbs.

Defense! That's what this Pokémon is all about. The growth on its head acts like a big shield that can protect Bastiodon from almost any attack. And although this Pokémon looks tough, there's a gentle nature under all that armor. Bastiodon can most often be found protecting the young Pokémon in its herd.

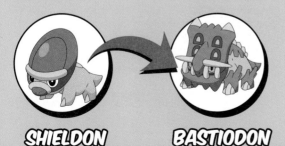

SHIELDON **BASTIODON**

BIBAREL

BEAVER POKÉMON

HOW TO SAY IT:
BEE-bear-ull

POSSIBLE MOVES:
Tackle, Growl, Defense Curl, Rollout, Water Sport, Headbutt, Hyper Fang, Yawn, Amnesia, Take Down, Super Fang, Superpower

TYPE:
Normal-Water

HEIGHT:
3' 03"

WEIGHT:
69.4 lbs.

Bibarel is the first Pokémon discovered with a Normal-and-Water-type combination. This Pokémon is comfortable on land and in rivers, where it's able to swim at pretty fast speeds. It uses its tail to build dams in rivers using trees or mud.

BIDOOF   BIBAREL

BIDOOF

PLUMP MOUSE POKÉMON

HOW TO SAY IT:
BEE-doof

POSSIBLE MOVES:
Tackle, Growl,
Defense Curl,
Rollout, Headbutt,
Hyper Fang,
Yawn, Amnesia,
Take Down,
Super Fang,
Superpower

TYPE:
Normal

HEIGHT:
1' 08"

WEIGHT:
44.1 lbs.

Don't be fooled by Bidoof's goofy appearance. This Pokémon has nerves of steel, and it can act quickly when danger is near. Bidoof constantly sharpens its super sharp teeth on trees and rocks.

BIDOOF   BIBAREL

BLISSEY

HAPPINESS POKÉMON

HOW TO SAY IT:
BLISS-see

POSSIBLE MOVES:
Pound, Growl, Tail Whip, Refresh, Softboiled, Doubleslap, Minimize, Sing, Egg Bomb, Defense Curl, Light Screen, Double-Edge, Fling, Healing Wish

TYPE: *Normal*

HEIGHT: *4' 11"*

Feeling low? Blissey knows just what to do to make you feel better. This sweet Pokémon can sense your sadness with its special fur. Then it will give you a bite of the egg in its pouch. This egg has an unusual power—it will make you feel caring and pleasant, and can nurture the sick back to health as well.

REMEMBER WHEN . . .
. . . we found out that Jessie of Team Rocket had a soft side? When Jessie visited a Pokémon Center she met a Blissey that she used to know in nursing school. Blissey remembered her old friend and gave Team Rocket some food, but got in trouble. Instead of running, Jessie stuck around to clear Blissey's name. And she didn't need a bite of egg to do it!

HAPPINY   CHANSEY   BLISSEY

BONSLY

HOW TO SAY IT:
BON-sleye
(rhymes with pie)

POSSIBLE MOVES:
Fake Tears,
Copycat, Flail,
Low Kick,
Rock Throw,
Mimic, Block,
Faint Attack,
Rock Tomb,
Rock Slide,
Slam,
Sucker Punch,
Double-Edge

TYPE:
Rock

HEIGHT:
1' 08"

WEIGHT:
33.1 lbs.

This cute little Pokémon may look like it's crying sometimes, but it's not sad. Its tears help regulate the water content of its body in dry places. Some people think Bonsly looks like a flower pot with a plant growing out of it. But those green things on top of its head are actually green rocks!

BONSLY   SUDOWOODO

BRONZONG

BRONZE BELL POKÉMON

HOW TO SAY IT:
brawn-ZONG

POSSIBLE MOVES:
Sunny Day, Rain
Dance, Tackle,
Confusion,
Hypnosis, Imprison,
Confuse Ray,
Extrasensory,
Iron Defense,
Safeguard, Block,
Gyro Ball, Future
Sight, Faint Attack,
Payback, Heal Block

TYPE:
Steel-Psychic

HEIGHT:
4' 03"

WEIGHT:
412.3 lbs.

Bronzong looks like a giant bell. When this bell rings, it doesn't mean the ice cream truck's in town—Bronzong can actually summon rain and sun! One Bronzong was found at a construction site after being asleep for two thousand years. Who knows what other mysterious powers it will reveal next?

BRONZOR   BRONZONG

BRONZOR

BRONZE POKÉMON

POSSIBLE MOVES:
*Tackle,
Confusion,
Hypnosis,
Imprison,
Confuse Ray,
Extrasensory,
Iron Defense,
Safeguard,
Gyro Ball,
Future Sight,
Faint Attack,
Payback,
Heal Block*

TYPE:
Steel-Psychic

HEIGHT:
1' 08"

WEIGHT:
133.4 lbs.

This odd Pokémon looks like a metal clock. Objects that resemble it have been unearthed in ancient tombs, but no one is sure if they are related. Scientists have tried to X-ray Bronzor to find out what makes it tick, but they haven't learned anything yet.

BRONZOR   **BRONZONG**

BUDEW

HOW TO SAY IT:
buh-DOO

POSSIBLE MOVES:
Absorb, Growth, Water Sport, Stun Spore, Mega Drain, Worry Seed

TYPE:
Grass-Poison

HEIGHT: 0' 08"

WEIGHT: 2.6 lbs.

Budew sure is cute, but if you have allergies, you'd better stay away! When Budew opens its bud, it spews out pollen that can make your nose run and your eyes water. You might be better off searching for Budew in winter, when it keeps its bud closed to stay warm.

BUDEW   ROSELIA   ROSERADE

BUIZEL

SEA WEASEL POKÉMON

HOW TO SAY IT:
BWEE-zuhl

POSSIBLE MOVES:
SonicBoom, Growl,
Water Sport, Quick
Attack, Water Gun,
Pursuit, Swift,
Aqua Jet, Agility,
Whirlpool,
Razor Wind

TYPE:
Water

HEIGHT:
2' 04"

WEIGHT:
65.0 lbs.

Buizel is a playful Pokémon that likes to splash around in water. The ring around its neck can inflate with air, like an inner tube. This allows Buizel to float with its head above water. When Buizel wants to swim, it deflates the ring.

BUIZEL   FLOATZEL

23

BUNEARY

HOW TO SAY IT:
buh-NEER-ree

POSSIBLE MOVES:
Splash, Pound, Defense Curl, Foresight, Endure, Frustration, Quick Attack, Jump Kick, Baton Pass, Agility, Dizzy Punch, Charm, Bounce, Healing Wish

TYPE:
Normal

HEIGHT:
1' 04"

WEIGHT:
12.1 lbs.

The long, furry ears on Buneary aren't just to make this little guy look adorable. Get too close, and Buneary will slam you with those ears! When Buneary's ears stand straight up, it means this Pokémon senses danger.

BUNEARY   LOPUNNY

BURMY (PLANT CLOAK)

HOW TO SAY IT:
BURR-mee

POSSIBLE MOVES:
Protect, Tackle,
Hidden Power

TYPE:
Bug

HEIGHT:
0' 08"

WEIGHT:
7.5 lbs.

Welcome to the weird world of Burmy! There are three different kinds of Burmy, depending on where you encounter them. This Burmy has a Plant Cloak. You will find this type of Burmy outdoors.

♀ (f)

♂ (m)

WORMADAM (PLANT CLOAK)

BURMY (PLANT CLOAK)

MOTHIM

25

BURMY (SANDY CLOAK)

BAGWORM POKÉMON

HOW TO SAY IT:
BURR-mee

POSSIBLE MOVES:
Protect, Tackle, Hidden Power

TYPE:
Bug

HEIGHT:
0' 08"

WEIGHT:
7.5 lbs.

You might find a Burmy with a Sandy Cloak hanging out inside a cave. Each Burmy covers itself with objects in its environment to stay warm. That's why this Burmy is protected by a skin of rocks and sand.

♀ WORMADAM (SANDY CLOAK)

♂ MOTHIM

BURMY (SANDY CLOAK)

BURMY (TRASH CLOAK)

HOW TO SAY IT:
BURR-mee

POSSIBLE MOVES:
*Protect, Tackle,
Hidden Power*

TYPE:
Bug

HEIGHT:
0' 08"

WEIGHT:
7.5 lbs.

You will find these pink Burmy inside buildings. Besides being pink, the Trash Cloak Burmy is like the other kinds of Burmy, with the same abilities. Like all Burmy, it can shed its skin and create a new one.

WORMADAM
(TRASH CLOAK)

BURMY
(TRASH CLOAK)

MOTHIM

CARNIVINE

BUG CATCHER POKÉMON

HOW TO SAY IT:
CAR-ni-vine

POSSIBLE MOVES:
Bind, Growth, Bite, Vine Whip, Sweet Scent, Ingrain, Faint Attack, Stockpile, Swallow, Spit Up, Crunch, Wring Out, Power Whip

TYPE:
Grass

HEIGHT:
4' 07"

WEIGHT:
59.5 lbs.

Carnivine likes to hang from tree branches by its tentacles. Then it uses its sweet-smelling saliva to lure prey. The prey gets close, and then . . . snap! Carnivine gobbles it up in its wide mouth.

DOES NOT EVOLVE

CASCOON

COCOON POKÉMON

HOW TO SAY IT:
cas-COON
POSSIBLE MOVES:
Harden
TYPE: *Bug*
HEIGHT: *2' 04"*
WEIGHT: *25.4 lbs.*

To a Cascoon, evolving into Dustox is its most important goal. When attacked, it won't retaliate because it wants to save energy for this evolution. But think twice before attacking this Pokémon— Cascoon know how to hold a grudge. When it does evolve into Dustox, it will seek revenge!

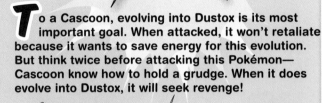

WURMPLE   **CASCOON**   **DUSTOX**

CHANSEY

EGG POKÉMON

HOW TO SAY IT:
CHANN-see
POSSIBLE MOVES:
Pound, Growl, Tail Whip, Refresh, Softboiled, Doubleslap, Minimize, Sing, Fling, Egg Bomb, Defense Curl, Light Screen, Double-Edge, Fling, Healing Wish
TYPE: *Normal*
HEIGHT: *3' 07"*
WEIGHT: *76.3 lbs.*

Like its evolved form, Blissey, Chansey carries an egg in its pouch. This special egg is nutritious and delicious. Chansey are not easy to find in the wild but you will often spot them working in Pokémon Centers with Nurse Joy.

HAPPINY   **CHANSEY**   **BLISSEY**

CHATOT

HOW TO SAY IT:
CHAH-tot

POSSIBLE MOVES:
Peck, Growl,
Mirror Move,
Sing, Fury Attack,
Chatter, Taunt,
Mimic, Roost,
Uproar,
Featherdance,
Hyper Voice

TYPE:
Normal-Flying

HEIGHT:
1' 08"

WEIGHT:
4.2 lbs.

Is Chatot another talking Pokémon, like Team Rocket's Meowth? Not exactly. Chatot can mimic human speech perfectly, but can't talk on its own. This Pokémon is musical, too, which may explain why its head and crest resemble a musical note. Chatot can swing its tail back and forth in perfect time, keeping the beat.

DOES NOT EVOLVE

CHERRIM

BLOSSOM POKÉMON

When the sun is out, Cherrim is always smiling! Though docile as a bud, this Pokémon cheerfully blooms during times of strong sunlight. But when the sun wanes, it turns back into a quiet, unassuming flower bud once again.

CHERUBI → CHERRIM

HOW TO SAY IT:
chuh-RIM

POSSIBLE MOVES:
Tackle, Growth, Leech Seed, Helping Hand, Magical Leaf, Sunny Day, Petal Dance, Worry Seed, Take Down, Solarbeam, Lucky Chant

TYPE: Grass

HEIGHT: 1' 08"

WEIGHT: 20.5 lbs.

CHERUBI

CHERRY POKÉMON

This little Pokémon is as sweet as a freshly ripe cherry! Cherubi likes to be in the sun, where it will become red and ripe. The tiny berry on its stem stores the nutrients it will need to evolve. When the berry wilts, Evolution is near.

CHERUBI → CHERRIM

HOW TO SAY IT:
chuh-ROO-bee

POSSIBLE MOVES:
Tackle, Growth, Leech Seed, Helping Hand, Magical Leaf, Sunny Day, Worry Seed, Take Down, Solarbeam, Lucky Chant, Solarbeam

TYPE: Grass

HEIGHT: 1' 04"

WEIGHT: 7.3 lbs.

CHIMCHAR

CHIMP POKÉMON

HOW TO SAY IT:
CHIM-charr

POSSIBLE MOVES:
Scratch, Leer, Ember, Taunt, Fury Swipes, Flame Wheel, Nasty Plot, Torment, Facade, Fire Spin, Slack Off, Flamethrower

TYPE:
Fire

HEIGHT:
1' 08"

WEIGHT:
13.7 lbs.

Meet Chimchar, the Fire-type starter Pokémon that Trainers can choose in the Sinnoh region. Like Charmander, Cyndaquil, and Torchic, Chimchar has some pretty cool Fire-type-attacks. A special fuel in Chimchar's stomach keeps the flame on the end of its tail lit, even in the rain. The only time the fire goes out is when Chimchar is sleeping.

CHIMCHAR　　　MONFERNO　　　INFERNAPE

CHIMECHO

WIND CHIME POKÉMON

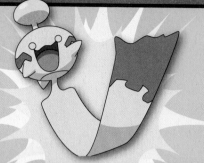

HOW TO SAY IT:
chy-MECK-ko

POSSIBLE MOVES:
Wrap, Growl, Astonish, Confusion, Uproar, Take Down, Yawn, Psywave, Double-Edge, Heal Bell, Safeguard, Extrasensory, Healing Wish

TYPE: Psychic
HEIGHT: 2' 00"
WEIGHT: 2.2 lbs.

Chimecho travels around by riding around on winds. When it wants to rest, it will attach itself to a tree branch of eaves of a building using the suction cup on top of its head.

CHINGLING   CHIMECHO

CHINGLING

BELL POKÉMON

HOW TO SAY IT:
CHING-ling

POSSIBLE MOVES:
Wrap, Growl, Astonish, Confusion, Uproar, Last Resort

TYPE: Psychic
HEIGHT: 0' 08"
WEIGHT: 1.3 lbs.

This Pokémon moves by lightly bouncing around. It makes a ringing sound every time it bounces. That ringing isn't just a pretty sound—Chingling can deafen an opponent with its high-frequency chimes.

CHINGLING   CHIMECHO

CLEFABLE

FAIRY POKÉMON

HOW TO SAY IT:
cluh-FAY-bull

POSSIBLE MOVES:
Sing, Doubleslap,
Minimize, Metronome

TYPE: Normal

HEIGHT: 4' 03"

WEIGHT: 88.2 lbs.

Clefable's pointy ears have excellent hearing. That's one reason why Clefable is so hard to find—they like to hide out, protecting their sensitive ears from loud noises.

CLEFFA   **CLEFAIRY**   **CLEFABLE**

CLEFAIRY

FAIRY POKÉMON

HOW TO SAY IT:
cluh-FAIR-ee

POSSIBLE MOVES:
Pound, Growl, Encore,
Sing, Doubleslap, Follow
Me, Minimize, Defense
Curl, Metronome, Cosmic
Power, Moonlight, Light
Screen, Meteor Mash,
Wakeup Slap, Lucky Chant,
Gravity, Healing Wish

TYPE: Normal

HEIGHT: 2' 00"

WEIGHT: 16.5 lbs.

Like Clefable, Clefairy is hard to find. Your best bet is to set out on the night of a full moon. Clefairy come out in large groups to play in the moonlight. It's quite an amazing sight!

CLEFFA   **CLEFAIRY**   **CLEFABLE**

CLEFFA

HOW TO SAY IT:
CLEFF-uh

POSSIBLE MOVES:
Pound, Charm, Encore, Sing, Sweet Kiss, Magical Leaf, Copycat

TYPE:
Normal

HEIGHT:
1' 00"

WEIGHT:
6.6 lbs.

Clefairy may be associated with the moon, but Cleffa like shooting stars best. They will come out at night to watch shooting stars streak across the night sky. They can also be found at sites where meteors have landed.

REMEMBER WHEN . . .
. . . Misty's Azurill made friends with a Cleffa? The little Pokémon was lost, but Misty and her friends returned it safely to its family.

CLEFFA   **CLEFAIRY**   **CLEFABLE**

COMBEE

HOW TO SAY IT:
COHM-bee

POSSIBLE MOVES:
Sweet Scent, Gust

TYPE:
Bug-Flying

HEIGHT:
1' 00"

WEIGHT:
12.1 lbs.

Combee looks like a single Pokémon made up of three Pokémon. Its body looks like pieces of a honeycomb. It spends its days collecting nectar for Vespiquen. At night, groups of Combee pile up in the hive to sleep.

COMBEE   VESPIQUEN

CRANIDOS

HEAD BUTT POKÉMON

HOW TO SAY IT:
CRANE-ee-dose

POSSIBLE MOVES:
*Headbutt, Leer,
Focus Energy,
Pursuit,
Take Down,
Scary Face,
Assurance,
AncientPower,
Zen Headbutt,
Screech,
Head Smash*

TYPE:
Rock

HEIGHT:
2' 11"

WEIGHT:
69.4 lbs.

This Pokémon used to live in dense jungles about 100 million years ago! Scientists revived it from a fossil that looked like an iron ball. That makes sense, since Cranidos has a skull as hard as iron! You definitely don't want to be on the receiving end of *that* headbutt!

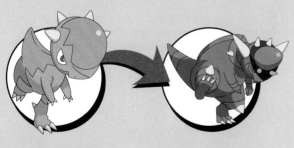

CRANIDOS   **RAMPARDOS**

CROAGUNK

TOXIC MOUTH POKÉMON

HOW TO SAY IT:
CROH-gunk

POSSIBLE MOVES:
Astonish, Mud-Slap, Poison Sting, Taunt, Pursuit, Faint Attack, Revenge, Swagger, Mud Bomb, Sucker Punch, Nasty Plot, Poison Jab, Sludge Bomb, Flatter

TYPE: Poison-Fighting

HEIGHT: 2' 04"

WEIGHT: 50.7 lbs.

This Pokémon is just oozing with poison! The pouches in its cheeks are filled with it. And if Croagunk touches a foe, the poison in its fingers will harm it.

CROAGUNK   TOXICROAK

CROBAT

BAT POKÉMON

HOW TO SAY IT:
CROH-bat

POSSIBLE MOVES:
Leech Life, Supersonic, Astonish, Bite, Wing Attack, Confuse Ray, Air Cutter, Mean Look, Poison Fang, Haze, Cross Poison, Screech, Air Slash

TYPE: Poison-Flying

HEIGHT: 5' 11"

WEIGHT: 165.3 lbs.

Look closely and you'll see that Crobat has an extra pair of wings. These wings allow Crobat to fly for long periods of time without resting. They also help Crobat fly really fast!

ZUBAT   GOLBAT   CROBAT

DIALGA

HOW TO SAY IT:
dee-AL-gah

POSSIBLE MOVES:
Dragonbreath,
Scary Face,
Metal Claw,
AncientPower,
Dragon Claw,
Roar of Time,
Heal Block,
Earth Power,
Slash, Flash
Cannon,
Aura Sphere

TYPE:
Steel-Dragon

HEIGHT:
17' 09"

WEIGHT:
1,505.8 lbs.

This Legendary Pokémon is the source of an old legend. The story goes that all time began to flow when Dialga was born. Dialga has the amazing ability to control time, so is it possible the legend is true? Only time will tell!

DOES NOT EVOLVE

DRAPION

OGRE SCORP POKÉMON

HOW TO SAY IT:
DRAPE-ee-ahn

POSSIBLE MOVES:
Thunder Fang, Ice Fang, Fire Fang, Bite, Poison Sting, Leer, Pin Missile, Acupressure, Knock Off, Scary Face, Toxic Spikes, Poison Fang, Crunch, Cross Poison

TYPE:
Poison-Dark

HEIGHT:
4' 03"

WEIGHT:
135.6 lbs.

Drapion is one tough Pokémon. Its body is covered with a hard, protective shell. Its powerful claws can rip up cars. Those same claws also secrete a powerful poison!

SKORUPI　　　DRAPION

DRIFBLIM

BLIMP POKÉMON

During the day, this Pokémon is half asleep, aimlessly floating around. At night, Drifblim gather in big groups and ride the winds—although no one is quite sure where they are going.

DRIFLOON   DRIFBLIM

DRIFLOON

BALLOON POKÉMON

HOW TO SAY IT:
DRIFF-loon

POSSIBLE MOVES:
Constrict, Minimize, Astonish, Gust, Focus Energy, Payback, Stockpile, Swallow, Spit Up, Ominous Wind, Baton Pass, Shadow Ball, Explosion

TYPE: Ghost-Flying

HEIGHT: 1' 04"

WEIGHT: 2.6 lbs.

Drifloon may look like a sweet balloon at first glance, but don't be fooled. This ghostly Pokémon is drawn to all things dark and eerie.

DRIFLOON   DRIFBLIM

DUSTOX

POISON MOTH POKÉMON

HOW TO SAY IT:
DUSS-tocks

POSSIBLE MOVES:
Confusion, Gust, Protect, Moonlight, Psybeam, Whirlwind, Light Screen, Silver Wind, Toxic, Bug Buzz

TYPE: Bug-Poison

HEIGHT: 3' 11"

WEIGHT: 69.7 lbs.

The best time to see a Dustox is at night. They are drawn to bright lights, like street lamps. Be careful not to scare or startle Dustox, though. It will release the highly toxic powder that coats its wings, which could make you really sick!

WURMPLE   CASCOON   DUSTOX

EMPOLEON

EMPEROR POKÉMON

HOW TO SAY IT:
im-PO-lee-on

POSSIBLE MOVES:
Tackle, Growl,
Bubble, Swords
Dance, Peck,
Metal Claw,
Swagger,
BubbleBeam,
Fury Attack,
Brine, Aqua Jet,
Whirlpool, Mist,
Drill Peck,
Hydro Pump

TYPE:
Water-Steel

HEIGHT:
5' 07"

WEIGHT:
186.3 lbs.

If you choose a Piplup as your starter Pokémon in the Sinnoh region, you can work toward evolving it into a powerful Empoleon. This Pokémon's sharp wings can slice through drifting ice. It can also swim faster than a jet ski!

PIPLUP   PRINPLUP   EMPOLEON

FEEBAS

FISH POKÉMON

HOW TO SAY IT:
FEE-bass

POSSIBLE MOVES:
Splash, Tackle, Flail

TYPE: Water

HEIGHT: 2' 00"

WEIGHT: 16.3 lbs.

Feebas isn't much to look at. It's ragged and tattered, and lives in ponds choked with weeds. Most Trainers ignore it, which is a mistake. A good Trainer knows that Feebas can be evolved into a gorgeous Milotic!

FEEBAS   **MILOTIC**

FINNEON

WING FISH POKÉMON

HOW TO SAY IT:
FINN-ee-ahn

POSSIBLE MOVES:
Pound, Water Gun, Rain Dance, Gust, Water Pulse, Captivate, Safeguard, Aqua Ring, Whirlpool, U-turn, Bounce, Silver Wind

TYPE: Water

HEIGHT: 1' 04"

WEIGHT: 15.4 lbs.

This Water-type Pokémon is best known for its good looks. When the sun hits the fins of its tail, it shines with a beautiful, deep color. Finneon also has a unique way of swimming. It flaps its two tail fins together, giving it the nickname "the Beautifly of the Sea."

FINNEON   **LUMINEON**

FLOATZEL

SEA WEASEL POKÉMON

Floatzel is a very helpful Pokémon. If it sees a swimmer struggling or drowning, it will go into rescue mode. When Floatzel floats on its back it resembles an inflatable boat. Its tail acts as a rudder, and the fins on its arms are like two oars. That's how Floatzel gets rescued swimmers safely back to shore.

HOW TO SAY IT:
FLOTE-zuhl

POSSIBLE MOVES:
Ice Fang, Growl, Water Sport, Quick Attack, Water Gun, Pursuit, Swift, Aqua Jet, Crunch, Agility, Whirlpool, Razor Wind, SonicBoom

TYPE: Water

HEIGHT: 3' 07"

WEIGHT: 73.9 lbs.

BUIZEL → FLOATZEL

GABITE

CAVE POKÉMON

This Pokémon prefers to live in dark caves, where it digs for valuable gems. Rumor has it that a Gabite cave holds a horde of these gems. But be warned—anyone venturing into Gabite's lair to steal treasure has never been seen or heard from again.

HOW TO SAY IT:
guh-BITE

POSSIBLE MOVES:
Tackle, Sand-Attack, Dragon Rage, Sandstorm, Take Down, Sand Tomb, Slash, Dragon Claw, Dig, Dragon Rush

TYPE: Dragon-Ground

HEIGHT: 4' 07"

WEIGHT: 123.5 lbs.

GIBLE → GABITE → GARCHOMP

GARCHOMP

MACH POKÉMON

HOW TO SAY IT:
gar-CHOMP

POSSIBLE MOVES:
Fire Fang, Tackle, Sand-Attack, Dragon Rage, Sandstorm, Take Down, Sand Tomb, Slash, Dragon Claw, Dig, Crunch, Dragon Rush, Sucker Punch, Payback, Dark Pulse

TYPE:
Dragon-Ground

HEIGHT:
6' 03"

WEIGHT:
209.4 lbs.

This fierce-looking Pokémon can fly at super speeds! When it folds up its body and extends its wings, it looks like a jet plane—and it can fly just as fast. Garchomp is so speedy that it's nearly impossible for any foe it targets to escape.

GIBLE　　　GABITE　　　GARCHOMP

GASTRODON (WEST SEA)

HOW TO SAY IT:
GASS-troh-dahn

POSSIBLE MOVES:
Mud-Slap, Mud Sport, Harden, Water Pulse, Mud Bomb, Hidden Power, Rain Dance, Body Slam, Muddy Water, Recover

TYPE: Water-Ground

HEIGHT: 2' 11"

WEIGHT: 65.9 lbs.

In the Sinnoh region, there are two types of Gastrodon. One can be found in the West, and the other can be found in the East. They look different, but otherwise they're basically the same.

SHELLOS (WEST SEA)   GASTRODON (WEST SEA)

GASTRODON (EAST SEA)

SEA SLUG POKÉMON

HOW TO SAY IT:
GASS-troh-dahn

POSSIBLE MOVES:
Mud-Slap, Mud Sport, Harden, Water Pulse, Mud Bomb, Hidden Power, Rain Dance, Body Slam, Muddy Water, Recover

TYPE: Water-Ground

HEIGHT: 2' 11"

WEIGHT: 65.9 lbs.

Gastrodon has a soft body, but it can heal any injuries it gets very quickly.

SHELLOS (EAST SEA)   GASTRODON (EAST SEA)

GASTLY

GAS POKÉMON

HOW TO SAY IT:
GAST-lee

POSSIBLE MOVES:
Hypnosis, Lick, Spite, Mean Look, Curse, Night Shade, Confuse Ray, Shadow Ball, Dream Eater, Destiny Bond, Nightmare

TYPE:
Ghost-Poison

HEIGHT: *4' 03"*

WEIGHT: *0.2 lbs.*

Gastly is one of the lightest Pokémon around, but that doesn't mean it doesn't have any power. The poison in its gaseous body is so powerful it can topple a foe of any size.

GASTLY   HAUNTER   GENGAR

GENGAR

SHADOW POKÉMON

HOW TO SAY IT:
GENN-garr

POSSIBLE MOVES:
Hypnosis, Lick, Spite, Mean Look, Curse, Night Shade, Confuse Ray, Shadow Ball, Dream Eater, Destiny Bond, Nightmare, Sucker Punch, Payback, Dark Pulse

TYPE:
Ghost-Poison

HEIGHT:
4' 11"

WEIGHT:
89.3 lbs.

*T*his menacing-looking Pokémon loves to travel in the shadows. Then it will leap out and strike its victims. One sign that Gengar is near is if there is a sudden chill in the air.

GASTLY   **HAUNTER**   **GENGAR**

GEODUDE

HOW TO SAY IT:
JEE-oh-dude

POSSIBLE MOVES:
Tackle, Defense Curl, Mud Sport, Rock Throw, Magnitude, Selfdestruct, Rollout, Rock Blast, Earthquake, Explosion, Double-Edge, Rock Polish, Stone Eye

TYPE: *Rock-Ground*

HEIGHT: *1' 04"*

WEIGHT: *44.1 lbs.*

Geodude like to live on mountains. At first glance, they look just like the rocks surrounding them. Be careful not to step on one by mistake!

GEODUDE   GRAVELER   GOLEM

GIBLE

LAND SHARK POKÉMON

HOW TO SAY IT:
GIBB-bull

POSSIBLE MOVES:
Tackle, Sand-Attack, Dragon Rage, Sandstorm, Take Down, Sand Tomb, Slash, Dragon Claw, Dig, Dragon Rush

TYPE: *Dragon-Ground*

HEIGHT: *2' 04"*

WEIGHT: *45.2 lbs.*

Gible like to hide out in small tunnels and caves. When prey is near, they jump out for a surprise attack.

GIBLE   GABITE   GARCHOMP

GIRAFARIG

LONG NECK POKÉMON

HOW TO SAY IT:
jer-AFF-uh-rigg

POSSIBLE MOVES:
Astonish, Tackle,
Growl, Confusion,
Odor Sleuth, Stomp,
Agility, Psybeam,
Baton Pass, Crunch,
Power Swap, Guard
Spec, Assurance,
Double Hit, Psychic,
Zen Headbutt

TYPE: Normal-Psychic

HEIGHT: 4' 11"

WEIGHT: 91.5 lbs.

This is one Pokémon you want to approach face-first! If you try to sneak up from behind, the tiny head on the end of Girafarig's tail will lash out and attack you. It's got a small brain but a big bite!

DOES NOT EVOLVE

GLAMEOW

CATTY POKÉMON

HOW TO SAY IT:
GLAM-ee-ow

POSSIBLE MOVES:
Fake Out, Scratch,
Growl, Hypnosis, Faint
Attack, Fury Swipes,
Charm, Assist,
Captivate, Slash,
Sucker Punch, Attract

TYPE: Normal

HEIGHT: 1' 08"

WEIGHT: 8.6 lbs.

This charming Pokémon has some quirky qualities. If you stare into its piercing eyes, you may fall into a hypnotic trance!

GLAMEOW   PURUGLY

GOLBAT

HOW TO SAY IT:
GOAL-bat

POSSIBLE MOVES:
Air Cutter, Mean Look, Poison Fang, Haze, Screech, Leech Life, Supersonic, Astonish, Bite, Wing Attack, Confuse Ray, Air Slash

TYPE: *Poison-Flying*

HEIGHT: *5' 03"*

WEIGHT: *121.3 lbs.*

This blood-sucking Pokémon flies around at night, searching for a fresh meal. It uses its sharp fangs to pierce its prey.

ZUBAT   GOLBAT   CROBAT

GOLDEEN

GOLDFISH POKÉMON

HOW TO SAY IT:
goal-DEEN

POSSIBLE MOVES:
Peck, Tail Whip, Water Sport, Supersonic, Horn Attack, Flail, Fury Attack, Waterfall, Horn Drill, Agility, Megahorn, Water Pulse, Aqua Ring

TYPE: *Water*

HEIGHT: *2' 00"*

WEIGHT: *33.1 lbs.*

With its billowing fins, Goldeen is one of the most beautiful Pokémon around. But that doesn't mean it's not tough. Its sharp horn can do serious damage!

GOLDEEN   SEAKING

GOLDUCK

HOW TO SAY IT:
GOAL-duck

POSSIBLE MOVES:
Scratch,
Water Sport,
Tail Whip,
Disable,
Confusion,
Fury Swipes,
Screech,
Psych Up,
Hydro Pump,
Water Pulse,
Zen Headbutt,
Amnesia

TYPE:
Water

HEIGHT:
5' 07"

WEIGHT:
168.9 lbs.

Golduck has two awesome qualities. First, it's able to swim at super speeds, powered by its long, strong wings. Golduck also has telekinetic powers. You can tell it's using them if the jewel on its forehead lights up.

REMEMBER WHEN . . .
. . . Ash battled a Trainer named Katie? Katie's Golduck beat Ash's Torkoal in battle. But Ash battled Katie again, and this time he used Corphish to take down Golduck.

PSYDUCK   **GOLDUCK**

53

GOLEM

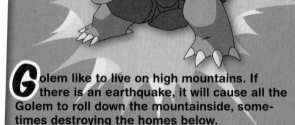

HOW TO SAY IT:
GO-lumm

POSSIBLE MOVES:
Tackle, Defense Curl, Mud Sport, Rock Throw, Magnitude, Selfdestruct, Rollout, Rock Blast, Earthquake, Explosion, Double-Edge, Rock Polish, Stone Edge

TYPE: Rock-Ground
HEIGHT: 4' 07"
WEIGHT: 661.4 lbs.

Golem like to live on high mountains. If there is an earthquake, it will cause all the Golem to roll down the mountainside, sometimes destroying the homes below.

GEODUDE   GRAVELER   GOLEM

GRAVELER

ROCK POKÉMON

HOW TO SAY IT:
GRAV-lerr

POSSIBLE MOVES:
Tackle, Defense Curl, Mud Sport, Rock Throw, Magnitude, Selfdestruct, Rollout, Rock Blast, Earthquake, Explosion, Double-Edge, Rock Polish, Stone Edge

TYPE: Rock-Ground
HEIGHT: 3' 03"
WEIGHT: 231.5 lbs.

A rock might not sound tasty to you, but a pile of pebbles is a Graveler's favorite meal! One Graveler can eat up to a ton of rocks a day. If a rock is covered in moss, that's an extra treat.

GEODUDE   GRAVELER   GOLEM

GROTLE

HOW TO SAY IT:
GRAH-tull

POSSIBLE MOVES:
Tackle, Withdraw, Absorb, Razor Leaf, Curse, Bite, Mega Drain, Leech Seed, Synthesis, Crunch, Giga Drain, Leaf Storm

TYPE:
Grass

HEIGHT:
3' 07"

WEIGHT:
213.8 lbs.

If you choose to start with a Grass-type in the Sinnoh region, you get a cute little Turtwig. Eventually, it could evolve into this tough-looking Grotle! Grotle likes to live in dark forests, but during the day it will come out to let the trees growing on its back get some sunshine.

TURTWIG   GROTLE   TORTERRA

GYARADOS

ATROCIOUS POKÉMON

HOW TO SAY IT:
GAIR-uh-dose

POSSIBLE MOVES:
Thrash, Bite, Dragon Rage, Leer, Twister, Rain Dance, Hydro Pump, Dragon Dance, Hyper Beam, Ice Fang, Aqua Tail

TYPE: Water-Flying

HEIGHT: 21' 04"

WEIGHT: 518.1 lbs.

No one looking at a sorry-looking Magikarp would ever imagine it evolves into mighty Gyarados! This vicious Pokémon has been known to destroy entire cities when it gets into a rage.

MAGIKARP   GYARADOS

HAPPINY

PLAYHOUSE POKÉMON

HOW TO SAY IT:
hap-PEE-nee

POSSIBLE MOVES:
Pound, Charm, Copycat, Refresh, Sweet Kiss

TYPE: Normal

HEIGHT: 2' 00"

WEIGHT: 53.8 lbs.

Isn't Happiny just the cutest thing? The object in its hands looks like an egg, but it's actually a stone. Happiny likes to pretend it's an egg, just like Chansey's.

HAPPINY   CHANSEY   BLISSEY

HAUNTER

GAS POKÉMON

You're walking down the street on a dark night. A figure beckons to you from the shadows. It's a Haunter! Don't go near it—it will lick you with its tongue, which is coated with deadly poison.

GASTLY → **HAUNTER** → **GENGAR**

HOW TO SAY IT:
HAWN-tuhr

POSSIBLE MOVES:
Hypnosis, Lick, Spite, Mean Look, Curse, Night Shade, Confuse Ray, Shadow Punch, Shadow Ball, Dream Eater, Destiny Bond, Nightmare, Sucker Punch, Payback, Dark Pulse

TYPE:
Ghost-Poison

HEIGHT: 5' 03"

WEIGHT: 0.2 lbs.

HERACROSS

SINGLE HORN POKÉMON

When it comes to brute strength, you can't beat Heracross! This Pokémon packs enough power to topple a big tree. It also can fling foes long distances with its curved horn.

DOES NOT EVOLVE

HOW TO SAY IT:
HERR-uh-cross

POSSIBLE MOVES:
Tackle, Leer, Horn Attack, Endure, Fury Attack, Brick Break, Counter, Take Down, Reversal, Night Slash, Aerial Ace, Close Combat, Feint, Megahorn

TYPE:
Bug-Fighting

HEIGHT: 4' 11"

WEIGHT: 119.0 lbs.

HIPPOPOTAS

HIPPO POKÉMON

HOW TO SAY IT:
HIP-po-puh-TOSS

POSSIBLE MOVES:
*Tackle, Sand-Attack,
Bite, Yawn,
Take Down,
Sand Tomb,
Crunch,
Earthquake,
Double-Edge,
Fissure*

TYPE:
Ground

HEIGHT:
2' 07"

WEIGHT:
109.1 lbs.

This Pokémon does not like to get wet! It doesn't even sweat. Instead, sand comes out of its pores. This sand keeps Hippopotas free of germs.

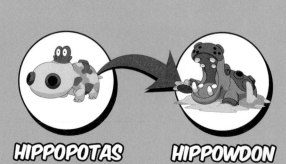

HIPPOPOTAS → **HIPPOWDON**

HIPPOWDON

HEAVYWEIGHT POKÉMON

HOW TO SAY IT:
hip-POW-donn

POSSIBLE MOVES:
Tackle,
Sand-Attack,
Bite, Yawn,
Ice Fang,
Thunder Fang,
Fire Fang,
Take Down,
Sand Tomb,
Crunch,
Earthquake,
Double-Edge,
Fissure

TYPE:
Ground

HEIGHT:
6' 07"

WEIGHT:
661.4 lbs.

Check out Hippowdon's big mouth! It can open as wide as a human basketball player! It can chomp down on a car and crush it with its massive jaws.

HIPPOPOTAS   **HIPPOWDON**

HONCHKROW

BIG BOSS POKÉMON

HOW TO SAY IT:
HONCH-kroh

POSSIBLE MOVES:
Astonish, Pursuit, Haze,
Wing Attack, Swagger,
Nasty Plot, Night Slash,
Dark Pulse

TYPE:
Dark-Flying

HEIGHT:
2' 11"

WEIGHT:
60.2 lbs.

This Pokémon likes to hang around with a lot of Murkrow. It makes them bring it food while it grooms its fancy feathers.

MURKROW **HONCHKROW**

HOOTHOOT

OWL POKÉMON

HOW TO SAY IT:
HOOT-HOOT

POSSIBLE MOVES: Tackle,
Growl, Foresight, Peck,
Hypnosis, Reflect, Take
Down, Confusion, Dream
Eater, Air Slash, Zen
Headbutt, Extrasensory,
Psycho Shift

TYPE:
Normal-Flying

HEIGHT:
2' 04"

WEIGHT:
46.7 lbs.

Hoothoot has an internal organ that can sense the world's rotation. That causes Hoothoot to hoot at the same time every day. Some Trainers will use this Pokémon as a clock!

HOOTHOOT **NOCTOW**

INFERNAPE

FLAME POKÉMON

HOW TO SAY IT:
inn-FUHR-nape

POSSIBLE MOVES:
Scratch, Leer, Ember, Taunt, Mach Punch, Fury Swipes, Flame Wheel, Feint, Punishment, Close Combat, Fire Spin, Calm Mind, Flare Blitz

TYPE:
Fire-Fighting

HEIGHT:
3' 11"

WEIGHT:
121.3 lbs.

Infernape is a quick and agile fighter. It can perform some complex moves using its hands and feet. The flame on its head gives it extra fire during battle. What's more, Infernape's flame will never go out!

CHIMCHAR　　　**MONFERNO**　　　**INFERNAPE**

KADABRA

HOW TO SAY IT:
kuh-DAB-ruh

POSSIBLE MOVES:
Teleport, Confusion, Psybeam, Reflect, Recover, Role Play, Psychic, Future Sight, Trick, Kinesis, Disable, Miracle Eye, Psycho Cut

TYPE:
Psychic

HEIGHT:
4' 03"

WEIGHT:
124.6 lbs.

Kadabra's psychic powers are so strong that its alpha waves can interfere with electronic equipment. Rumor has it that its eerie shadow sometimes appears on TV screens. If you see Kadabra's shadow, change the channel! It's supposed to be bad luck.

ABRA   KADABRA   ALAKAZAM

KRICKETOT

CRICKET POKÉMON

HOW TO SAY IT:
CRICK-eh-tot

POSSIBLE MOVES:
Growl, Bide

TYPE:
Bug

HEIGHT:
1' 00"

WEIGHT:
4.9 lbs.

Kricketot has a special way of communicating with others in its species. It shakes its head back and forth, rubbing its feelers together. Fans of Kricketot say the sound is truly poetic.

KRICKETOT   KRICKETUNE

KRICKETUNE

CRICKET POKÉMON

HOW TO SAY IT:
CRICK-eh-toon

POSSIBLE MOVES:
Growl, Bide, Fury Cutter, Leech Life, Sing, Focus Energy, X-Scissor, Screech, Big Buzz, Perish Song

TYPE:
Bug

HEIGHT:
3' 03"

WEIGHT:
56.2 lbs.

Kricketune has more sophisticated attacks than its pre-evolved form, Kricketot. It also makes more sophisticated music. To express its emotions, Kricketune composes beautiful melodies.

KRICKETOT   **KRICKETUNE**

LOPUNNY

RABBIT POKÉMON

HOW TO SAY IT:
LAH-pun-nee

POSSIBLE MOVES:
Pound, Defense Curl, Foresight, Endure, Return, Quick Attack, Mirror Coat, Magic Coat, Splash, Jump Kick, Baton Pass, Agility, Dizzy Punch, Charm, Bounce, Healing Wish

TYPE:
Normal

HEIGHT:
3' 11"

WEIGHT:
73.4 lbs.

The fluffy white fur at the end of Lopunny's ears can cover up its whole body when danger is near. Lopunny likes to take good care of this fur, and in general is very neat and tidy.

BUNEARY ➔ LOPUNNY

LUCARIO

AURA POKÉMON

HOW TO SAY IT:
loo-CAR-ee-oh

POSSIBLE MOVES:
*Quick Attack,
Foresight, Detect,
Metal Claw, Counter,
Force Palm, Feint,
Bone Rush, Metal
Sound, Me First,
Swords Dance,
Aura Sphere, Close
Combat, Dark Pulse,
Dragon Pulse,
Extremespeed*

TYPE:
Fighting-Steel

HEIGHT:
3' 11"

WEIGHT:
119.0 lbs.

Lucario possesses some unusual powers. This Pokémon can understand human speech. It can also read thoughts and movements of all living things due to its ability to sense and catch the auras of others.

RIOLU   LUCARIO

LUMINEON

Lumineon lives deep in the sea. When it wants to lure prey, the patterns on its four fins will light up. It uses the two small fins on its chest to crawl along the ocean floor.

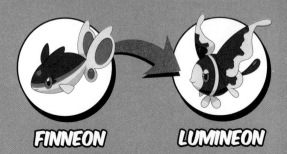

FINNEON   LUMINEON

LUXIO

HOW TO SAY IT:
LUCKS-ee-oh

POSSIBLE MOVES:
Tackle, Leer,
Charge, Bite,
Spark, Roar,
Swagger,
Crunch,
Thunder Fang,
Scary Face,
Discharge

TYPE:
Electric

HEIGHT:
2' 11"

WEIGHT:
67.2 lbs.

Luxio like to live in groups. They communicate by putting their front legs together. They express emotion with the rhythm of the electrical charges that pulse from their claws. That same electricity can also be used in attacks during a Pokémon battle.

SHINX   LUXIO   LUXRAY

LUXRAY

GLEAM EYES POKÉMON

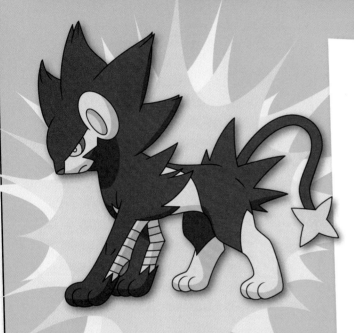

HOW TO SAY IT:
LUCKS-ray

POSSIBLE MOVES:
*Tackle, Leer,
Charge, Bite,
Spark, Roar,
Swagger,
Crunch,
Thunder Fang,
Scary Face,
Discharge*

TYPE:
Electric

HEIGHT:
4' 07"

WEIGHT:
92.6 lbs.

This Electric-type Pokémon has X-ray vision! When its eyes flash, it can see through objects. That comes in handy when Luxray is searching for hidden prey.

SHINX   **LUXIO**   **LUXRAY**

MACHAMP

HOW TO SAY IT:
mah-CHAMP

POSSIBLE MOVES: *Low Kick, Leer, Focus Energy, Karate Chop, Foresight, Seismic Toss, Revenge, Vital Throw, Submission, Cross Chop, Scary Face, Dynamic Punch, Wakeup Slap*

TYPE: *Fighting*

HEIGHT: *5' 03"*

WEIGHT: *286.6 lbs.*

For this Fighting-type Pokémon, four arms are definitely better than two! Machamp can deliver 1,000 punches in just two seconds! Its arms are strong as well as speedy. Machamp can pick up an opponent and toss it over the horizon.

MACHOP **MACHOKE** **MACHAMP**

MACHOKE

SUPERPOWER POKÉMON

HOW TO SAY IT:
mah-CHOKE

POSSIBLE MOVES: *Low Kick, Leer, Focus Energy, Karate Chop, Foresight, Seismic Toss, Revenge, Vital Throw, Submission, Cross Chop, Scary Face, Dynamic Punch, Wakeup Slap*

TYPE: *Fighting*

HEIGHT: *4' 11"*

WEIGHT: *155.4 lbs.*

This muscular Pokémon boasts such super strength that it can't control it. That's why Machoke wears the belt around its waist. Without the belt, Machoke would be unstoppable!

MACHOP **MACHOKE** **MACHAMP**

MACHOP

SUPERPOWER POKÉMON

This little Pokémon isn't as strong as its evolved forms, but it's still super tough. What it lacks in size, it makes up in skill. Machop trains in many different forms of martial arts all day long.

MACHOP   **MACHOKE**   **MACHAMP**

HOW TO SAY IT:
mah-CHOP
POSSIBLE MOVES:
Low Kick, Leer, Focus Energy, Karate Chop, Foresight, Seismic Toss, Revenge, Vital Throw, Submission, Cross Chop, Scary Face, Dynamic Punch, Wakeup Slap
TYPE: Fighting
HEIGHT: 2' 07"
WEIGHT: 43.0 lbs.

MAGIKARP

FISH POKÉMON

Magikarp is a terrible swimmer. It has pathetic moves. That's why it's considered to be the weakest Pokémon ever! But if you're a patient Trainer, you'll end up with a powerful Gyarados when it evolves.

MAGIKARP   **GYARADOS**

HOW TO SAY IT:
MADG-eh-karp
POSSIBLE MOVES:
Splash, Tackle, Flail
TYPE:
Water
HEIGHT:
2' 11"
WEIGHT:
22.0 lbs.

MANAPHY

HOW TO SAY IT:
MAN-uh-fee

POSSIBLE MOVES:
Tail Glow, Bubble,
Water Sport,
Charm, Supersonic,
Bubblebeam, Acid
Armor, Whirlpool,
Water Pulse, Aqua
Ring, Dive, Rain
Dance, Heart Swap

TYPE:
Water

HEIGHT:
1' 00"

WEIGHT:
3.1 lbs.

This Legendary Pokémon has a body made up of 80% water. Most of its attacks are Water-type attacks. But Manaphy's most interesting attack is a Psychic-type attack called Heart Swap. Manaphy can enter the body of another Pokémon or human. On the battlefield, Manaphy can use this attack to switch healing effects with its opponent.

DOES NOT EVOLVE

MANTINE

HOW TO SAY IT:
MAN-teen

POSSIBLE MOVES:
Tackle, Bubble, Supersonic, Bubblebeam, Take Down, Agility, Wing Attack, Water Pulse, Confuse Ray, Psybeam, Bullet Seed, Signal Beam, Headbutt, Bounce, Aqua Ring, Hydro Pump

TYPE:
Water-Flying

HEIGHT:
6' 11"

WEIGHT:
485.0 lbs.

Mantine love to swim in the open seas in big groups. Sometimes Remoraid will hitch a ride to scavenge for Mantine's leftovers. Mantine doesn't mind this at all.

MANTYKE **MANTINE**

MANTYKE

HOW TO SAY IT:
MAN-tike

POSSIBLE MOVES:
Tackle, Bubble,
Supersonic,
Bubblebeam,
Headbutt, Agility,
Wing Attack, Water
Pulse, Take Down,
Confuse Ray,
Bounce,
Aqua Ring,
Hydro Pump

TYPE:
Water-Flying

HEIGHT:
3' 03"

WEIGHT:
143.3 lbs.

This friendly Pokémon loves humans. Scientists have studied the patterns on its back. They can tell what region Mantyke is from depending on the pattern.

MANTYKE   MANTINE

MARILL

AQUA MOUSE POKÉMON

Cute and happy Marill can stay safe in any storm. How? The tip of its tail contains oil that is lighter than water, keeping Marill afloat no matter how rough the waters. Think of it as Marill's built-in life preserver!

HOW TO SAY IT:
MARE-ill

POSSIBLE MOVES:
Tackle, Defense Curl, Tail Whip, Water Gun, Rollout, Bubblebeam, Double-Edge, Rain Dance, Hydro Pump, Aqua Ring, Aqua Tail

TYPE: Water
HEIGHT: 1' 04"
WEIGHT: 18.7 lbs.

AZURILL   MARILL   AZUMARILL

MEDICHAM

MEDITATE POKÉMON

Shhhh. If you want your Medicham to be its best, give it plenty of quiet time to meditate. It is how Medicham gains a sixth sense to know what move its opponents will make. Combine its Psychic abilities with quick and dance-like moves, and you've got a Pokémon that is hard to beat!

HOW TO SAY IT:
MED-uh-cham

POSSIBLE MOVES:
Fire Punch, Ice Punch, Bide, Meditate, Confusion, Detect, Hidden Power, Mind Reader, Calm Mind, Hi Jump Kick, Psych Up, Reversal, Recover, Feint, Force Palm, Thunderpunch,

TYPE: Fighting-Psychic
HEIGHT: 4' 03"
WEIGHT: 69.4 lbs.

MEDITITE   MEDICHAM

MEDITITE

HOW TO SAY IT:
MED-uh-tite

POSSIBLE MOVES:
Bide, Meditate,
Confusion, Detect,
Hidden Power,
Mind Reader,
Calm Mind,
Hi Jump Kick,
Psych Up,
Reversal,
Recover,
Power Trick,
Force Palm

TYPE:
Fighting-Psychic

HEIGHT:
2' 00"

WEIGHT:
24.7 lbs.

If you are looking for a Meditite, you will most likely find one meditating. Every day, this Psychic-type spends hours each day deep in thought and practicing yoga. It only eats one berry a day. This practice helps its spirit become tempered and sharp.

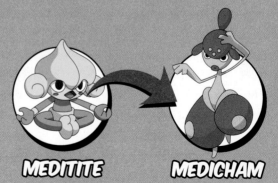

MEDITITE → MEDICHAM

MESPRIT

EMOTION POKÉMON

HOW TO SAY IT:
MESS-prit

POSSIBLE MOVES:
Rest, Imprison,
Protect,
Confusion,
Lucky Chant,
Future Sight,
Charm,
Extrasensory,
Copycat,
Natural Gift,
Healing Wish

TYPE:
Psychic

HEIGHT:
1' 00"

WEIGHT:
0.7 lbs.

Legendary Pokémon alert! Magical, mysterious, and powerful, Mesprit was said to have taught humans the pain of sorrow as well as the pleasures of joy. This unusual Pokémon slumbers at the bottom of a lake. But it is believed that Mesprit's spirit can leave its body to travel on the water's surface.

DOES NOT EVOLVE

MILOTIC

TENDER POKÉMON

HOW TO SAY IT:
my-LOW-tick

POSSIBLE MOVES:
Water Gun, Wrap,
Water Sport,
Refresh, Water
Pulse, Twister,
Recover, Rain
Dance, Hydro
Pump, Attract,
Safeguard,
Captivate,
Aqua Tail,
Aqua Ring

TYPE:
Water

HEIGHT:
20' 04"

WEIGHT:
357.1 lbs.

Fighting with a friend? If Milotic is nearby, your anger will be washed away by its ability to bring soothing calm to fighting people. Milotic is considered to be one of the most beautiful Pokémon in the world!

FEEBAS   MILOTIC

MIME JR.

MIME POKÉMON

HOW TO SAY IT:
mime-JOON-yerr

POSSIBLE MOVES:
Tickle, Barrier, Confusion, Copycat, Meditate, Encore, Doubleslap, Mimic, Light Screen, Reflect, Psybeam, Substitute, Recycle, Trick, Psychic, Role Play, Baton Pass, Safeguard

TYPE:
Psychic

HEIGHT:
2' 00"

WEIGHT:
28.7 lbs.

This little creature likes to dance and joke around. The pre-evolved version of Mr. Mime is also helpful in a battle. Mime Jr. can weaken any attack used against it!

MIME JR.   MR. MIME

MISDREAVUS

SCREECH POKÉMON

HOW TO SAY IT:
miss-DREE-vuss

POSSIBLE MOVES:
Growl, Psywave, Spite,
Astonish, Confuse Ray,
Mean Look, Psybeam,
Pain Split, Perish Song,
Grudge, Payback,
Shadow Ball

TYPE: Ghost

HEIGHT: 2' 04"

WEIGHT: 2.2 lbs.

A spooky wailing fills the air. Chills run up and down your body. Suddenly, something yanks your hair! It can only be one Pokémon, the trouble-making Misdreavus. This Ghost Pokémon loves to sneak up on people and scare them just to watch their reactions.

MISDREAVUS   MISMAGIUS

MISMAGIUS

MAGICAL POKÉMON

HOW TO SAY IT:
miss-MAJ-ee-us

POSSIBLE MOVES:
Lucky Chant, Magical
Leaf, Growl, Psywave,
Spite, Astonish

TYPE: Ghost

HEIGHT: 2' 11"

WEIGHT: 9.7 lbs.

W hen Misdreavus evolves into Mismagius, its pranks turn more powerful. You'll get more than just a scare when Mismagius casts a spell on you. If you are unlucky, you'll suffer from headaches and hallucinations. But if Mismagius likes you, it can cast spells of happiness on you!

MISDREAVUS   MISMAGIUS

MONFERNO

HOW TO SAY IT:
mon-FIR-noh

POSSIBLE MOVES:
Scratch,
Leer,
Ember,
Taunt,
Mach Punch,
Fury Swipes,
Flame Wheel,
Feint, Torment,
Close Combat,
Fire Spin,
Slack Off,
Flare Blitz

TYPE:
Fire-Fighting

HEIGHT:
2' 11"

WEIGHT:
48.5 lbs.

If you started out with a Chimchar and trained it well, you'll end up with Monferno. Monferno may look playful, but unless you like your bananas well done, stand back from this tough Fire-and-Fighting-type Pokémon. The flame on its tail is one of Monferno's biggest weapons. And this Pokémon knows how to use it!

CHIMCHAR   MONFERNO   INFERNAPE

MOTHIM

HOW TO SAY IT:
MAH-thim

POSSIBLE MOVES:
Tackle, Protect, Hidden Power, Confusion, Gust, Poisonpowder, Psybeam, Camouflage, Silver Wind, Air Slash, Psychic, Big Buzz

TYPE:
Bug-Flying

HEIGHT:
2' 11"

WEIGHT:
51.4 lbs.

Mothim flies free, flitting around the countryside searching for its favorite flower honey. It doesn't mind snatching honey from the adorable Combee if it needs to. Mothim, evolved from Burmy, are unique because they are all males. Wormadam is the female Evolution of Burmy.

BURMY
(TRASH CLOAK)

BURMY
(SANDY CLOAK)

BURMY
(PLANT CLOAK)

MOTHIM

MR. MIME

HOW TO SAY IT:
MISS-tur MIME

POSSIBLE MOVES:
Barrier, Confusion, Doubleslap, Light Screen, Reflect, Magical Leaf, Encore, Psybeam, Trick, Role Play, Psychic, Baton Pass, Power Swap, Guard Spec, Copycat, Meditate, Mimic, Substitute, Recycle, Future Site

TYPE: *Psychic*

HEIGHT: *4' 03"*

WEIGHT: *120.1 lbs.*

Not only can Mr. Mime create walls out of thin air, it also can make objects real by pantomiming the shape with its hands. Once you believe it exists, it becomes real!

MIME JR.   **MR. MIME**

MUNCHLAX

HOW TO SAY IT:
MUNCH-lacks

POSSIBLE MOVES:
Metronome, Odor Sleuth, Tackle, Defense Curl, Amnesia, Lick, Recycle, Screech, Stockpile, Swallow, Body Slam, Fling, Rollout, Natural Gift, Last Resort

TYPE: *Normal*

HEIGHT: *2' 00"*

WEIGHT: *231.5 lbs.*

Feed me! If it could speak, that's what Munchlax would tell you. This hungry little Pokémon loves to gobble huge amounts of food in one gulp. Who can blame it? Munchlax has got a lot of eating to do if it wants to evolve into the larger-than-life Snorlax!

MUNCHLAX   **SNORLAX**

MURKROW

HOW TO SAY IT:
MURR-kroh

POSSIBLE MOVES:
Peck, Astonish, Pursuit, Haze, Night Shade, Repeat, Faint Attack, Taunt, Mean Look, Wing Attack, Assurance, Sucker Punch

TYPE: *Dark-Flying*

HEIGHT: *1' 08"*

WEIGHT: *4.6 lbs.*

Murkow's got a bad rap as an unlucky Pokémon. Many people believe seeing a Murkrow will bring misfortune your way. We don't know if that is true, but maybe we shouldn't feel too bad for this sneaky Pokémon. It loves shiny things so much that it steals rings and other jewelry from people.

MURKROW   HONCHKROW

NOCTOWL

HOW TO SAY IT:
NOCKT-owl

POSSIBLE MOVES:
Tackle, Growl, Foresight, Peck, Hypnosis, Reflect, Take Down, Confusion, Dream Eater, Sky Attack, Air Slash, Zen Headbutt, Extrasensory, Psycho Shift, Roost

TYPE: *Normal-Flying*

HEIGHT: *5' 03"*

WEIGHT: *89.9 lbs.*

Battling in the dark? That's not a problem when you've got Noctowl on your team! This Pokémon's sharp eyes can see in very little light. Even better, Noctowl won't make a sound as it flaps its wings. It can sneak up and surprise an opponent day or night!

HOOTHOOT   NOCTOWL

OCTILLERY

JET POKÉMON

HOW TO SAY IT:
ock-TILL-uh-ree

POSSIBLE MOVES:
Rock Blast, Water Gun, Constrict, Psybeam, Aurora Beam, Bubblebeam, Focus Energy, Octazooka, Bullet Seed, Wring Out, Signal Beam, Ice Beam, Hyper Beam

TYPE: Water

HEIGHT: 2' 11"

WEIGHT: 62.8 lbs.

Once Octillery grabs onto you with your tentacles, you are stuck! The suction-cups on the end will make it hard to wiggle free. But that's not the only trick Octillery has. It can also use its rock-hard head to deliver a stunning blow!

REMORAID → OCTILLERY

ONIX

ROCK SNAKE POKÉMON

HOW TO SAY IT:
ON-icks

POSSIBLE MOVES:
Tackle, Screech, Bind, Rock Throw, Rage, Slam, Harden, Mud Sport, Rock Tomb, Sandstorm, Dragonbreath, Iron Tail, Sand Tomb, Double-Edge, Stone Edge, Rock Polish

TYPE: Rock-Ground

HEIGHT: 28' 10"

WEIGHT: 463.0 lbs.

Powerful Onix feels most at home underground. It can tunnel through the ground at speeds of 50 mph. It will never lose direction because a magnet in its brain acts like an internal compass.

ONIX → STEELIX

PACHIRISU

ELESQUIRREL POKÉMON

HOW TO SAY IT:
patch-ee-REE-su

POSSIBLE MOVES:
Growl, Bide, Quick
Attack, Charm,
Spark, Endure,
Swift, Sweet Kiss,
Discharge, Super
Fang, Last Resort

TYPE:
Electric

HEIGHT:
1' 04"

WEIGHT:
8.6 lbs.

Does Pikachu have some competition? It looks like there is a new adorable Electric-type Pokémon on the block! Pachirisu like to live in the treetops. In fact, that is where the Pokémon likes to store its favorite snack – berries! Just like Pikachu, Pachirisu generates electricity in its cheeks and then releases it from its tail.

DOES NOT EVOLVE

PALKIA

SPACIAL POKÉMON

HOW TO SAY IT:
PAL-kee-uh

POSSIBLE MOVES:
Dragonbreath,
Scary Face,
Water Pulse,
AncientPower,
Dragon Claw,
Spatial Rend,
Heal Block,
Earth Power,
Slash, Aqua Tail,
Aura Sphere,
Rock Polish

TYPE:
Water-Dragon

HEIGHT:
13' 09"

WEIGHT:
740.8 lbs.

Like other Legendary Pokémon, Palkia has amazing powers. This big and scary Water-and-Dragon-type can distort space. Many myths and legends in the Sinnoh are about this mysterious Pokémon. Will you be able to unlock its secrets?

DOES NOT EVOLVE

PELIPPER

WATER BIRD POKÉMON

HOW TO SAY IT:
PELL-uh-purr

POSSIBLE MOVES:
Growl, Water Gun, Water Sport, Supersonic, Wing Attack, Mist, Protect, Stockpile, Swallow, Spit Up, Hydro Pump, Water Pulse, Payback, Roost, Fling, Tail Wind

TYPE: *Water-Flying*

HEIGHT: *3' 11"*

WEIGHT: *61.7 lbs.*

Pelipper just fills its massive bill with whatever it wants to carry and takes off flying. It will even give small Pokémon a ride in its huge mouth. To rest, Pelipper bobs on the ocean waves.

WINGULL　　**PELIPPER**

PICHU

TINY MOUSE POKÉMON

HOW TO SAY IT:
PEE-choo

POSSIBLE MOVES:
Thundershock, Charm, Tail Whip, Thunder Wave, Sweet Kiss, Feint, Discharge

TYPE: *Electric*

HEIGHT: *1' 00"*

WEIGHT: *4.4 lbs.*

Electrifying things come in tiny packages! Although Pichu is small, it carries quite a punch. Pichu is not very skilled at controlling its electricity. It often discharges accidentally. So be very careful, keep your Pichu happy, and one day it may evolve into a Pikachu!

PICHU　　**PIKACHU**　　**RAICHU**

PIKACHU

We all know Ash's best friend, Pikachu. But if you want to catch one in the wild, you might run into the same kind of problems that Ash did when he first met Pikachu. These Electric-types are very smart and quick to anger. Approach carefully and watch out for those lightning bolts!

PICHU   PIKACHU   RAICHU

HOW TO SAY IT:
PEE-ka-choo

POSSIBLE MOVES:
Thundershock, Growl, Tail Whip, Thunder Wave, Quick Attack, Double Team, Slam, Thunderbolt, Light Screen, Thunder, Agility, Feint, Discharge

TYPE: *Electric*

HEIGHT: *1' 04"*

WEIGHT: *13.2 lbs.*

PIPLUP

PENGUIN POKÉMON

You can choose to start your adventure in Sinnoh with a Piplup. If you like your Pokémon cute yet powerful, Piplup is the one for you! A great swimmer, this Water-type Pokémon can dive into cold waters to look for food. It is also a very proud Pokémon and hates accepting food from people.

PIPLUP   PRINPLUP   EMPOLEON

HOW TO SAY IT:
PIP-lup

POSSIBLE MOVES:
Pound, Growl, Bubble, Water Sport, Peck, Bide, Bubblebeam, Fury Attack, Brine, Whirlpool, Mist, Drill Peck, Hydro Pump

TYPE: *Water*

HEIGHT: *1' 04"*

WEIGHT: *11.5 lbs.*

PONYTA

FIRE HORSE POKÉMON

HOW TO SAY IT:
POH-nee-tah

POSSIBLE MOVES:
Quick Attack, Growl,
Tail Whip, Ember,
Stomp, Fire Spin,
Take Down, Agility,
Bounce, Fire Blast,
Tackle, Flare Blitz

TYPE: Fire

HEIGHT: 3' 03"

WEIGHT: 66.1 lbs.

If a Ponyta is galloping toward you, get out of the way! Although Ponyta is light and fast on its feet, its hooves are ten times harder than diamonds. Anything Ponyta tramples on will be flattened out in no time!

PONYTA   RAPIDASH

PRINPLUP

PENGUIN POKÉMON

HOW TO SAY IT:
PRIN-plup

POSSIBLE MOVES:
Tackle, Growl, Bubble,
Water Sport, Peck, Metal
Claw, Bide, Bubblebeam,
Fury Attack, Brine,
Whirlpool, Mist, Drill
Peck, Hydro Pump

TYPE: Water

HEIGHT: 2' 07"

WEIGHT: 50.7 lbs.

When cute little Piplup evolves, it becomes the strong and tough Prinplup. And Prinplup just doesn't look strong – this Water-type Pokémon can prove it by snapping a tree trunk in half with its wings!

PIPLUP   PRINPLUP   EMPOLEON

PSYDUCK

DUCK POKÉMON

HOW TO SAY IT:
SYE-duck

POSSIBLE MOVES:
Water Sport, Scratch,
Tail Whip, Disable,
Confusion, Screech,
Psych Up, Fury Swipes,
Hydro Pump, Water Gun,
Water Pulse, Amnesia,
Zen Headbutt, Attract

TYPE: Water

HEIGHT: 2' 07"

WEIGHT: 43.2 lbs.

This confused and bewildered Pokémon almost always has a headache, making it hard for it to think. When the headache becomes unbearable, Psyduck can let loose some strange and amazing powers!

PSYDUCK → GOLDUCK

PURUGLY

TIGER CAT POKÉMON

HOW TO SAY IT:
purr-UG-lee

POSSIBLE MOVES:
Fake Out, Scratch,
Growl, Hypnosis,
Faint Attack,
Fury Swipes,
Charm, Assist,
Captivate, Slash,
Swagger, Body Slam,

TYPE: Normal

HEIGHT: 3' 03"

WEIGHT: 96.6 lbs.

Purugly certainly believes it is something special! It will walk right into the homes of other Pokémon and find the most comfortable spot to sleep. To scare off enemies, Purugly will wrap its forked tail around its body tightly to make itself look bigger.

GLAMEOW → PURUGLY

QUAGSIRE

WATER FISH POKÉMON

HOW TO SAY IT:
KWAG-sire

POSSIBLE MOVES:
Amnesia, Yawn, Earthquake, Rain Dance, Mist, Haze, Tail Whip, Mud Sport, Mud Shot, Slam, Mud Bomb, Muddy Water

TYPE:
Water-Ground

HEIGHT:
4' 07"

WEIGHT:
165.3 lbs.

Chill out and take it easy with the carefree Quagsire! This Pokémon is so easygoing that it doesn't mind when it bumps its head into boats or the river bottom. In fact, Quagsire is so mellow that it just hangs out with its mouth wide-open in the water, just waiting for food to swim on in!

WOOPER → QUAGSIRE

RAICHU

MOUSE POKÉMON

HOW TO SAY IT:
RYE-choo

POSSIBLE MOVES:
Thundershock, Tail Whip, Quick Attack, Thunderbolt

TYPE: Electric

HEIGHT: 2' 07"

WEIGHT: 66.1 lbs.

Raichu is the evolved form of Pikachu. Its electric charges can reach 100,000 volts. That's enough juice to make a Gyarados faint! If Raichu stores too much electricity, it can get cranky, so it needs to release the extra energy out through its tail.

PICHU → PIKACHU → RAICHU

RAMPARDOS

HOW TO SAY IT:
ram-PAR-dose

POSSIBLE MOVES:
Headbutt, Leer,
Focus Energy,
Pursuit,
Take Down,
Scary Face,
Assurance,
AncientPower,
Endeavor,
Zen Headbutt,
Screech,
Head Smash

TYPE:
Rock

HEIGHT:
5' 03"

WEIGHT:
226.0 lbs.

The evolution of the ancient Pokémon Cranidos, Rampardos can headbutt like no other Pokémon! If this Pokémon lowers its head to charge at you, run for your life! Its iron skull can shatter anything in one hit.

CRANIDOS   RAMPARDOS

93

RAPIDASH

FIRE HORSE POKÉMON

HOW TO SAY IT:
RAP-id-dash

POSSIBLE MOVES:
Growl, Tail Whip, Ember, Stomp, Fire Spin, Take Down, Agility, Fury Attack, Bounce, Fire Blast, Poison Jab, Megahorn, Quick Attack, Flare Blitz

TYPE: *Fire*

HEIGHT: *5' 07"*

WEIGHT: *209.4 lbs.*

Ponyta is fast, but when it evolves into Rapidash don't blink or you'll miss it! Rapidash can run at speeds of 150 miles per hour. Its hooves barely touch the ground as it zooms through the countryside.

PONYTA **RAPIDASH**

REMORAID

JET POKÉMON

HOW TO SAY IT:
REM-or-aid

POSSIBLE MOVES:
Water Gun, Lock-on, Psybeam, Aurora Beam, Bubblebeam, Focus Energy, Ice Beam, Hyper Beam, Bullet Seed, Water Pulse, Signal Beam

TYPE: *Water*

HEIGHT: *2' 00"*

WEIGHT: *26.5 lbs.*

Remoraid might hitch a ride on Mantine, but this feisty little fish can fend for itself! You could say it even has the best aim of any Pokémon ever. It shoots water out of its mouth to bring down flying prey. The accurate Remoraid can hit a target from more than 300 feet away!

REMORAID **OCTILLERY**

RIOLU

HOW TO SAY IT:
ree-OH-loo

POSSIBLE MOVES:
Quick Attack, Foresight, Endure, Counter, Force Palm, Feint, Reversal, Screech, Copycat

TYPE:
Fighting

HEIGHT:
2' 04"

WEIGHT:
44.5 lbs.

This tough and determined Pokémon won't let anything stop it. It will march all night, crossing mountains and valleys to get where it needs to go. Riolu can find others of its kind by sending out pulses from its body. If it needs help, other Riolu will come running!

RIOLU   LUCARIO

95

ROSELIA

THORN POKÉMON

HOW TO SAY IT:
roh-ZELL-ee-ah

POSSIBLE MOVES:
Absorb, Growth, Poison Sting, Stun Spore, Mega Drain, Leech Seed, Magical Leaf, Grasswhistle, Giga Drain, Sweet Scent, Ingrain, Toxic, Petal Dance, Aromatherapy, Synthesis, Toxic Spikes

TYPE:
Grass-Poison

HEIGHT:
1' 00"

WEIGHT:
4.4 lbs.

Please don't pick the flowers! If you try to grab one of Roselia's blooms, you'll be looking for a bandage. The pretty Pokémon shoots sharp thorns at anyone trying to steal its flowers. The thorns on Roselia's head are even more dangerous. They contain a strong poison.

BUDEW   **ROSELIA**   **ROSERADE**

ROSERADE

HOW TO SAY IT:
ROSE-raid

POSSIBLE MOVES:
Weather Ball,
Poison Sting,
Mega Drain,
Magical Leaf,
Sweet Scent

TYPE:
Grass-Poison

HEIGHT:
2' 11"

WEIGHT:
32.0 lbs.

Be careful! The beautiful and sweet-smelling Roserade hides a nasty surprise. Its bouquet-like arms are covered with sharp, poisonous thorns on the inside. Roserade moves gracefully with dancer-like movements, shooting out its thorns as it whirls.

BUDEW → ROSELIA → ROSERADE

97

SEAKING

GOLDFISH POKÉMON

HOW TO SAY IT:
SEE-king

POSSIBLE MOVES:
Peck, Tail Whip, Water Sport, Supersonic, Horn Attack, Flail, Fury Attack, Waterfall, Horn Drill, Agility, Megahorn, Poison Jab, Water Pulse, Aqua Ring

TYPE:
Water

HEIGHT:
4' 03"

WEIGHT:
86.0 lbs.

When Seaking gather together during spawning season, it is quite a beautiful sight. Large groups of them swim up streams and rivers, coloring the waters a brilliant red. But Seaking have more going for them than just looks. The sharp horn on Seaking's head is very useful. Not only can it be helpful in a battle, but it can also be used to drill holes into boulders.

REMEMBER WHEN . . .
. . . Ash and Misty entered the annual Seaking catching competition? The winner would be awarded a year's supply of chocolate for catching the biggest Seaking. Misty tied for first with a Trainer named Andreas. They had to battle to decide the winner. Misty took home the trophy – and shared the chocolate.

GOLDEEN   SEAKING

SHELLOS (EAST SEA)

SEA SLUG POKÉMON

HOW TO SAY IT:
SHELL-oss

POSSIBLE MOVES:
Mud-Slap,
Mud Sport,
Harden, Water
Pulse, Mud Bomb,
Hidden Power,
Rain Dance, Body
Slam, Muddy
Water, Recover

TYPE:
Water

HEIGHT:
1' 00"

WEIGHT:
13.9 lbs.

Your Shellos could look very different from someone else's. It all depends on where you catch it! If you snagged your Shellos in the east, it will be a blue and greenish color with horn-like ears.

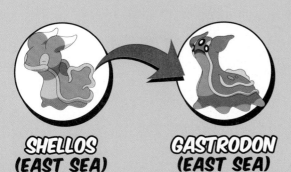

SHELLOS
(EAST SEA)

GASTRODON
(EAST SEA)

SHELLOS (WEST SEA)

HOW TO SAY IT:
SHELL-oss

POSSIBLE MOVES:
Mud-Slap, Mud Sport, Harden, Water Pulse, Mud Bomb, Hidden Power, Rain Dance, Body Slam, Muddy Water, Recover

TYPE:
Water

HEIGHT:
1' 00"

WEIGHT:
13.9 lbs.

If you found your Shellos in the west, it will be pink and white with a spiky back. These colors and body shape are better suited for its surroundings near the waters of the West Sea.

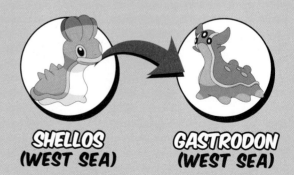

SHELLOS (WEST SEA) GASTRODON (WEST SEA)

SHIELDON

SHIELD POKÉMON

HOW TO SAY IT:
SHEEL-dahn

POSSIBLE MOVES:
Tackle, Protect, Taunt, Metal Sound, Take Down, Iron Defense, Swagger, AncientPower, Endure, Metal Burst, Iron Head

TYPE:
Rock-Steel

HEIGHT:
1' 08"

WEIGHT:
125.7 lbs.

Shieldon once lived in dense jungles about 100 million years ago. Cloned from a fossil, you can now own a Shieldon today! This Pokémon can face any danger head on with its hard-as-a-rock face. But this Pokémon is very vulnerable to attacks from behind. If you want to catch one, try sneaking up on it!

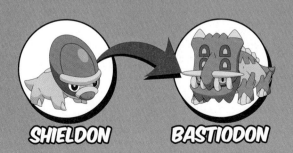

SHIELDON   BASTIODON

SHINX

HOW TO SAY IT:
SHINKS

POSSIBLE MOVES:
*Tackle, Leer,
Charge, Bite,
Spark, Roar,
Swagger, Crunch,
Thunder Fang,
Scary Face,
Discharge*

TYPE:
Electric

HEIGHT:
1' 08"

WEIGHT:
20.9 lbs.

Try to grab this adorable Electric-type Pokémon and its entire body will flash with a bright light! You'll be temporarily blinded, and Shinx will scamper away. Its front legs generate all the electricity that Shinx needs.

SHINX → **LUXIO** → **LUXRAY**

SILCOON

COCOON POKÉMON

If you own a Wurmple and it evolves, you could end up with Silcoon! Silcoon is not a very active Pokémon. In fact, all it will do is attach itself to a tree and sit patiently until it evolves into the lovely Beautifly. Now that's something worth waiting for!

WURMPLE → SILCOON → BEAUTIFLY

HOW TO SAY IT:
sill-COON

POSSIBLE MOVES:
Harden

TYPE:
Bug

HEIGHT:
2' 00"

WEIGHT:
22.0 lbs.

SKORUPI

SCORPION POKÉMON

If a Skorupi grabs onto you with the claw on its tail, you are in big trouble. It will not let go until it injects its poison and you begin to feel the effects. Be very careful walking through the desert or other sandy places. Skorupi digs holes in the sand and hides in them to wait for its prey.

SKORUPI → DRAPION

HOW TO SAY IT:
sco-ROO-pee

POSSIBLE MOVES:
Bite, Poison Sting, Leer, Pin Missile, Acupressure, Knock Off, Scary Face, Toxic Spikes, Poison Fang, Crunch, Cross Poison

TYPE: *Poison-Bug*

HEIGHT: *2' 07"*

WEIGHT: *26.5 lbs.*

SKUNTANK

SKUNK POKÉMON

HOW TO SAY IT:
SKUHN-tank

POSSIBLE MOVES:
Scratch, Focus Energy, Poison Gas, Screech, Fury Swipes, Smokescreen, Toxic, Slash, Night Slash, Flamethrower, Memento, Explosion

TYPE:
Poison-Dark

HEIGHT:
3' 03"

WEIGHT:
83.8 lbs.

Hold your nose! The evolved form of Stunky, Skuntank is even smellier than its predecessor. Don't think running away will help. Skuntank can shoot a foul smelling secretion from the tip of its tail at targets over 160 feet away!

STUNKY   SKUNTANK

SNEASEL

SHARP CLAW POKÉMON

Will Sneasel ever stop being so sneaky? This thief loves nothing better than climbing trees and stealing eggs. Sometimes it will even scare Pidgey out of their nests.

SNEASEL → WEAVILE

HOW TO SAY IT:
SNEE-sull
POSSIBLE MOVES:
Scratch, Leer, Taunt, Quick Attack, Faint Attack, Fury Swipes, Agility, Icy Wind, Slash, Beat Up, Metal Claw, Screech, Ice Shard
TYPE: Dark-Ice
HEIGHT: 2' 11"
WEIGHT: 61.7 lbs.

SNORLAX

SLEEPING POKÉMON

Snorlax, when it's not sleeping, will gobble nearly 900 pounds of food every day. In fact, the only time you'll find Snorlax awake is when it is eating! Children like to use the belly of this lazy, sweet Pokémon as a trampoline.

MUNCHLAX → SNORLAX

HOW TO SAY IT:
SNORE-lacks
POSSIBLE MOVES:
Tackle, Amnesia, Defense Curl, Belly Drum, Yawn, Rest, Snore, Body Slam, Block, Rollout, Lick, Sleep Talk, Crunch, Giga Impact
TYPE: Normal
HEIGHT: 6' 11"
WEIGHT: 1,014.1 lbs.

SNOVER

FROST TREE POKÉMON

HOW TO SAY IT:
SNOH-verr

POSSIBLE MOVES:
Powder Snow, Leer, Razor Leaf, Icy Wind, Grasswhistle, Swagger, Mist, Ice Shard, Ingrain, Wood Hammer, Blizzard, Sheer Cold

TYPE: Ice-Grass

HEIGHT: 3' 03"

WEIGHT: 111.3 lbs.

Snover is at home on snow-covered mountains, where it can keep away from humans. This unusual Pokémon will grow berries on its body during the springtime.

SNOVER   ABOMASNOW

STEELIX

IRON SNAKE POKÉMON

HOW TO SAY IT:
STEE-licks

POSSIBLE MOVES:
Screech, Rock Throw, Rage, Dragonbreath, Sandstorm, Slam, Iron Tail, Crunch, Double-Edge, Thunder Fang, Ice Fang, Mud Sport, Tackle, Harden, Bind, Rock Tomb, Rock Polish, Stone Edge

TYPE: Steel-Ground

HEIGHT: 30' 02"

WEIGHT: 881.8 lbs.

Gold may be valuable, but nothing is more precious to a Pokémon Trainer than an experienced Steelix. The strong Pokémon has a body harder than any metal.

ONIX   STEELIX

SPIRITOMB

FORBIDDEN POKÉMON

HOW TO SAY IT:
SPEER-i-toom

POSSIBLE MOVES:
Curse, Pursuit, Confuse Ray, Spite, Shadow Sneak, Faint Attack, Hypnosis, Dream Eater, Ominous Wind, Sucker Punch, Nasty Plot, Memento, Dark Pulse

TYPE:
Ghost-Dark

HEIGHT:
3' 03"

WEIGHT:
238.1 lbs.

Definitely creepy, and more than a little freaky, Spiritomb is one spooky Pokémon. It is said that Spiritomb was created from 108 evil spirits. Over 500 years ago, it was punished for its bad deeds by being sealed into the cracks of the odd keystone.

DOES NOT EVOLVE

STARAPTOR

PREDATOR POKÉMON

HOW TO SAY IT:
star-RAP-torr

POSSIBLE MOVES:
Tackle, Growl, Quick Attack, Wing Attack, Double Team, Endeavor, Whirlwind, Aerial Ace, Take Down, Close Combat, Agility, Brave Bird

TYPE:
Normal-Flying

HEIGHT:
3' 11"

WEIGHT:
54.9 lbs.

It's hard to believe that the final evolutionary stage of the adorable Starly is the fierce Staraptor! This Pokémon knows no fear. It will boldly challenge foes that are much bigger than itself. Powerful and strong, Staraptor can grasp other Pokémon in its claws and fly away with them.

STARLY → STARAVIA → STARAPTOR

STARAVIA

STARLING POKÉMON

HOW TO SAY IT:
star-AY-vee-uh

POSSIBLE MOVES:
Tackle, Growl, Quick Attack, Wing Attack, Double Team, Endeavor, Whirlwind, Aerial Ace, Take Down, Agility, Brave Bird

TYPE:
Normal-Flying

HEIGHT:
2' 00"

WEIGHT:
34.2 lbs.

Hold your Bug-type Pokémon close when a flock of Staravia flies by! Staravia hunt in the forests and plains they call home for Bug-type Pokémon. They live in flocks and are very territorial. If two groups of Staravia meet up, it means trouble!

STARLY STARAVIA STARAPTOR

STARLY

STARLING POKÉMON

HOW TO SAY IT:
STAR-lee

POSSIBLE MOVES:
Tackle, Growl,
Quick Attack,
Wing Attack,
Double Team,
Endeavor,
Whirlwind,
Aerial Ace,
Take Down,
Agility,
Brave Bird

TYPE:
Normal-Flying

HEIGHT:
1' 00"

WEIGHT:
4.4 lbs.

Tiny Starly is the beginning of an evolutionary chain of tough Flying-type Pokémon! You'll find Starly living in large flocks. But you'll probably hear Starly before you see it. It is very noisy and always chattering. Even though Starly is small, it has very strong wings.

STARLY   STARAVIA   STARAPTOR

STUNKY

SKUNK POKÉMON

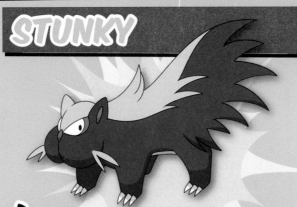

If you smell something stinky, chances are a Stunky is around! It shoots out a foul-smelling secretion when it is in danger. The horrible stench can linger for over 24 hours! The nasty stink alone is enough to keep enemies far, far away from Stunky.

STUNKY **SKUNTANK**

HOW TO SAY IT:
STUN-kee

POSSIBLE MOVES:
Scratch, Focus Energy, Poison Gas, Screech, Fury Swipes, Smokescreen, Toxic, Slash, Night Slash, Memento, Explosion

TYPE: Poison-Dark

HEIGHT: 1' 04"

WEIGHT: 42.3 lbs.

SUDOWOODO

IMITATION POKÉMON

Look closely at Sudowoodo. It looks like a tree, but it's not! This Rock-type Pokémon disguises itself as a tree to avoid enemies. If you touch its body you'll find it is made of rock, not wood!

BONSLY **SUDOWOODO**

HOW TO SAY IT:
soo-doh-WOOD-oh

POSSIBLE MOVES:
Rock Throw, Mimic, Flail, Low Kick, Rock Slide, Block, Faint Attack, Slam, Double-Edge, Wood Hammer, Copycat, Rock Tomb, Sucker Punch, Hammer Arm

TYPE: Rock

HEIGHT: 3' 11"

WEIGHT: 83.8 lbs.

TENTACOOL

JELLYFISH POKÉMON

HOW TO SAY IT:

TEN-ta-cool

POSSIBLE MOVES:

Poison Sting, Supersonic, Constrict, Acid, Bubblebeam, Wrap, Barrier, Screech, Hydro Pump, Toxic Spikes, Water Pulse, Poison Jab, Wring Out

TYPE: *Water-Poison*

HEIGHT: *2' 11"*

WEIGHT: *100.3 lbs.*

Tentacool are hard to see as they float along with the ocean waves. Sometimes you don't notice one is around until you feel it sting you with its tentacles!

TENTACOOL   TENTACRUEL

TENTACRUEL

JELLYFISH POKÉMON

HOW TO SAY IT:

TEN-ta-crool

POSSIBLE MOVES:

Poison Sting, Screech, Hydro Pump, Supersonic, Constrict, Acid, Toxic Spikes, Bubblebeam, Wrap, Barrier, Water Pulse, Poison Jab, Wring Out

TYPE: *Water-Poison*

HEIGHT: *5' 03"*

WEIGHT: *121.3 lbs.*

Tentacruel has a web of 80 lethal tentacles that it uses to wrap around its enemies and sting them. Beware the large red orb on Tentacruel's head. It will glow before it shoots out a harsh ultrasonic blast!

TENTACOOL   TENTACRUEL

TORTERRA

CONTINENT POKÉMON

HOW TO SAY IT:
tor-TERR-uh

POSSIBLE MOVES:
Tackle, Withdraw, Absorb, Razor Leaf, Wood Hammer, Curse, Bite, Mega Drain, Earthquake, Leech Seed, Synthesis, Crunch, Giga Drain, Leaf Storm

TYPE:
Grass-Ground

HEIGHT:
7' 03"

WEIGHT:
683.4 lbs.

If you chose Turtwig to start your adventures in the Sinnoh region, you might end up with a Torterra! The final evolutionary form of Turtwig, Torterra is one enormous Pokémon. If you think the forest has come alive and is moving, you are probably witnessing herds of Torterra migrating.

TURTWIG   **GROTLE**   **TORTERRA**

113

TOXICROAK

TOXIC MOUTH POKÉMON

HOW TO SAY IT:
TOCKS-eh-croke

POSSIBLE MOVES:
Astonish, Mud-Slap, Poison Sting, Taunt, Pursuit, Faint Attack, Revenge, Swagger, Mud Bomb, Sucker Punch, Nasty Plot, Poison Jab, Sludge Bomb, Flatter

TYPE:
Poison-Fighting

HEIGHT:
4' 03"

WEIGHT:
97.9 lbs.

Toxicroak is the evolved form of Croagunk. It packs one powerful poisonous punch! The Pokémon transports powerful poison from its pouches to the spikes on its fists. Even a small scratch can cause a lot of damage.

CROAGUNK   TOXICROAK

114

TURTWIG

TINY LEAF POKÉMON

Turtwig is one of the three starter Pokémon in the Sinnoh region. Even though Turtwig is a Grass-type Pokémon, you'll find that this little guy likes to live close to water. The shell on its back grows even stronger when it absorbs water. If Turtwig becomes thirsty, the leaf on the top of its head will wilt!

TURTWIG   **GROTLE**   **TORTERRA**

HOW TO SAY IT:
TUR-twig
POSSIBLE MOVES:
Tackle, Withdraw, Absorb, Razor Leaf, Curse, Bite, Mega Drain, Leech Seed, Synthesis, Crunch, Giga Drain, Leaf Storm
TYPE:
Grass
HEIGHT:
1' 04"
WEIGHT:
22.5 lbs.

UNOWN

SYMBOL POKÉMON

HOW TO SAY IT:
un-OWN
POSSIBLE MOVES:
Hidden Power
TYPE:
Psychic
HEIGHT:
1' 08"
WEIGHT:
11.0 lbs.

You can find the mysterious Unown on walls, shaped like ancient writing. There are many different types of Unown and it is believed they each have different abilities. While many have studied these baffling Pokémon, none have the answers. Maybe you can crack the code of the Unown?

DOES NOT EVOLVE

UXIE

HOW TO SAY IT:
YUKE-see

POSSIBLE MOVES:
Rest, Imprison, Endure, Confusion, Yawn, Future Sight, Amnesia, Extrasensory, Flail, Natural Gift, Memento

TYPE:
Psychic

HEIGHT:
1' 00"

WEIGHT:
0.7 lbs.

Uxie is just one new Legendary Pokémon that can be found in Sinnoh. You may have spotted this elusive Pokémon and don't even remember. That is because Uxie can erase your memory! This Psychic-type Pokémon is thought to be extremely wise.

DOES NOT EVOLVE

VESPIQUEN

HOW TO SAY IT:
VES-pa-kween

POSSIBLE MOVES:
Sweet Scent, Gust, Poison Sting, Confuse Ray, Fury Cutter, Defend Order, Pursuit, Fury Swipes, Power Gem, Heal Order, Toxic, Slash, Captivate, Attack Order, Swagger, Destiny Bond

TYPE:
Bug-Flying

HEIGHT:
3' 11"

WEIGHT:
84.9 lbs.

When Combee evolves into Vespiquen, its body becomes a hive for baby Combee. A Vespiquen is like a flying nursery! Baby Combee live on honey in Vespiquen's hive. If Vespiquen is in trouble, it sends the babies out of the hive to attack any enemies.

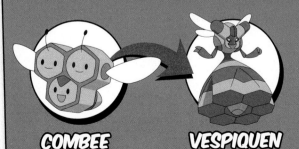

COMBEE   VESPIQUEN

WEAVILE

SHARP CLAW POKÉMON

HOW TO SAY IT:
WEE-vile

POSSIBLE MOVES:
Embargo, Revenge, Assurance, Scratch, Leer, Taunt, Quick Attack, Screech, Faint Attack, Fury Swipes, Nasty Plot, Icy Wind, Night Slash, Fling, Metal Claw, Dark Pulse

TYPE: Dark-Ice

HEIGHT: 3' 07"

WEIGHT: 75.0 lbs.

If you are walking through a snowy forest and see mysterious patterns carved on trees or on ice surfaces, you might bump into a Weavile! This Dark-and-Ice-type Pokémon uses its super-sharp claws to carve out messages to other Weavile.

SNEASEL → WEAVILE

WHISCASH

WHISKERS POKÉMON

HOW TO SAY IT:
WISS-cash

POSSIBLE MOVES:
Tickle, Mud-Slap, Mud Sport, Water Sport, Water Gun, Magnitude, Amnesia, Rest, Snore, Earthquake, Future Sight, Fissure, Zen Headbutt, Aqua Tail

TYPE: Water-Ground

HEIGHT: 2' 11"

WEIGHT: 52.0 lbs.

Whiscash can cause a massive earthquake by thrashing about. It can also predict real earthquakes. If Whiscash gets angry and goes on a rampage, you can feel the tremors up to three miles away!

BARBOACH → WHISCASH

WINGULL

SEAGULL POKÉMON

Wingull flies high, riding on the ocean winds as if it were a glider. This crafty Pokémon uses its beak to carry valuables until it can hide them away.

HOW TO SAY IT:
WIN-gull

POSSIBLE MOVES:
Growl, Water Gun, Supersonic, Wing Attack, Mist, Quick Attack, Pursuit, Agility

TYPE: Water-Flying

HEIGHT: 2' 00"

WEIGHT: 20.9 lbs.

WINGULL   PELIPPER

WOOPER

WATER FISH POKÉMON

Happy little Wooper spend most of their time in the water. These Water-and-Ground-type Pokémon don't mind the cold. You'll find them living in chilly waters.

HOW TO SAY IT:
WOO-purr

POSSIBLE MOVES:
Water Gun, Tail Whip, Mud Shot, Slam, Amnesia, Earthquake, Rain Dance, Mist, Haze

TYPE: Water-Ground

HEIGHT: 1' 04"

WEIGHT: 18.7 lbs.

WOOPER   QUAGSIRE

WORMADAM (PLANT CLOAK)

BAGWORM POKÉMON

HOW TO SAY IT:
WURR-mah-dam

POSSIBLE MOVES:
Tackle, Protect, Hidden Power, Confusion, Razor Leaf, Growth, Psybeam, Captivate, Flail, Psychic, Attract, Leaf Storm

TYPE:
Bug-Grass

HEIGHT:
1' 08"

WEIGHT:
14.3 lbs.

The unusual Evolution of Wormadam all starts with a Burmy. If you own a female Burmy, you'll get a Wormadam when it evolves. But what kind of Wormadam will it be? There are three possible choices. If your Burmy has a Plant Cloak, then you will end up with a Wormadam with a Plant Cloak!

**BURMY
(PLANT CLOAK)**   **WORMADAM
(PLANT CLOAK)**

WORMADAM (SANDY CLOAK)

HOW TO SAY IT:
WURR-mah-dam

POSSIBLE MOVES:
Tackle, Protect, Hidden Power, Confusion, Rock Blast, Harden, Psybeam, Captivate, Flail, Psychic, Attract, Fissure

TYPE:
Bug-Ground

HEIGHT:
1' 08"

WEIGHT:
14.3 lbs.

Your Ground-type Wormadam will come ready to battle with lots of possible attacks! If you want a Wormadam with a Sandy Cloak, make sure your Burmy has one, too.

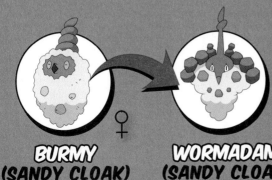

BURMY
(SANDY CLOAK)

WORMADAM
(SANDY CLOAK)

WORMADAM (TRASH CLOAK)

BAGWORM POKÉMON

HOW TO SAY IT:
WURR-mah-dam

POSSIBLE MOVES:
Tackle, Protect,
Hidden Power,
Confusion,
Mirror Shot,
Metal Sound,
Psybeam,
Captivate,
Flail, Psychic,
Attract,
Iron Head

TYPE:
Bug-Steel

HEIGHT:
1' 08"

WEIGHT:
14.3 lbs.

If you're dreaming of a Steel-type Wormadam, make sure your Burmy has a Trash Cloak. Once Burmy has evolved, it cannot change types. When Burmy evolves into Wormadam, its coat becomes a part of its body.

**BURMY
(TRASH CLOAK)** **WORMADAM
(TRASH CLOAK)**

WURMPLE

HOW TO SAY IT:
WURM-pull

POSSIBLE MOVES:
Tackle,
String Shot,
Poison Sting,
Haze, Air Slash

TYPE:
Bug

HEIGHT:
1' 00"

WEIGHT:
7.9 lbs.

One small Pokémon, two big choices. What will your Wurmple become? It could evolve into a Cascoon before transforming into Dustox. It could also evolve into a Silcoon and then into a stunning Beautifly!

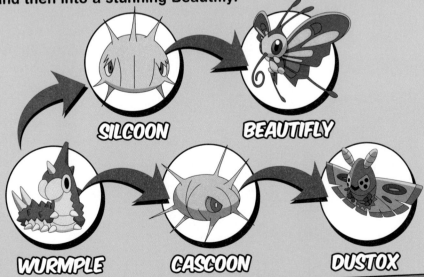

SILCOON   BEAUTIFLY

WURMPLE   CASCOON   DUSTOX

123

ZUBAT

BAT POKÉMON

HOW TO SAY IT:
ZOO-bat

POSSIBLE MOVES:
Leech Life,
Supersonic,
Astonish, Bite,
Wing Attack,
Confuse Ray,
Air Cutter,
Mean Look,
Poison Fang,
Haze, Air Slash

TYPE:
Poison-Flying

HEIGHT:
2' 07"

WEIGHT:
16.5 lbs.

Zubat is most at home during the night or in shadowy places. How can this Pokémon fly around in the dark? It emits ultrasonic waves that bounce off any object in its way. Zubat like to live in large colonies. You can find them hanging upside down in caves or under the eaves of houses.

ZUBAT   GOLBAT   CROBAT

ASH

Ash was only going to bring Pikachu along on his journey to Sinnoh, but Aipom didn't want to be left behind, and snuck onto the ship! After Ash reached Sinnoh, he captured Starly and Turtwig. Then, during a battle with Team Rocket, Starly evolved into Staravia.

PIKACHU
PAGE 89

STARAVIA
PAGE 109

TURTWIG
PAGE 115

AIPOM
PAGE 10

BROCK

As everyone knows, Brock is a Rock-type Trainer. As the Gym Leader in Pewter City, he handed out the Boulder Badge. But during his travels in Sinnoh, he's made room for Croagunk, a fierce Poison-and-Fighting-type Pokémon.

SUDOWOODO
PAGE 111

CROAGUNK
PAGE 38

DAWN

When Dawn began her Sinnoh journey with Piplup, the little Pokémon was not always obedient. But Dawn eventually won Piplup's trust, and is fast becoming a great Coordinator with two other cute Pokémon: Buneary and Pachirisu.

BUNEARY
PAGE 24

PIPLUP
PAGE 89

PACHIRISU
PAGE 86